I0545946

Steele and Stone

by

Kay Phoenix

The Daring Hearts Series

This is a work of fiction. Names, characters, places, and incidents are either the product of the author's imagination or are used fictitiously, and any resemblance to actual persons living or dead, business establishments, events, or locales, is entirely coincidental.

Steele and Stone

COPYRIGHT © 2016 by Kay Phoenix

All rights reserved. No part of this book may be used or reproduced in any manner whatsoever without written permission of the author or The Wild Rose Press, Inc. except in the case of brief quotations embodied in critical articles or reviews.
Contact Information: info@thewildrosepress.com

Cover Art by *Kristian Norris*

The Wild Rose Press, Inc.
PO Box 708
Adams Basin, NY 14410-0708
Visit us at www.thewildrosepress.com

Publishing History
First Champagne Rose Edition, 2016
Print ISBN 978-1-5092-1071-8
Digital ISBN 978-1-5092-1072-5

The Daring Hearts Series
Published in the United States of America

"How are you feeling today?"

a familiar voice asked behind him. He didn't have to turn to know who it was, but he turned anyway, temporarily forgetting about his sunburn until he saw the shocked expression on her face.

"Whoa! No sunblock either? I had some, you could have asked," she said. "That'll peel for sure."

Blue! Brilliant, shimmering blue eyes. He hadn't seen her eyes during their hike, as they'd been hidden behind sunglasses the whole time, and he'd always been a sucker for blue eyes. She wore jeweled sandals, torn jeans and a lime green, long-sleeved shirt with a misshapen Buddha on it, protruding outward over her breasts. Her warm blonde hair hung long, loose, and wavy as she leaned casually against the doorframe.

"I see you've already made yourself quite at home here," she said. "Randall told me he let you use the conference room."

"What are you doing here?" he asked, in a tone that sounded a bit too firm.

"Oh, no 'how are you' or 'nice to see you'?" She tilted her head to the side, causing a loose curl to graze her breast.

He turned back to the coffee, adding cream and stirring absently. "I didn't mean to sound rude. You just surprised me."

Praise for Kay Phoenix

"I loved Michael and Elle's emotional journey of learning to let go in order to love again."

~*Beverly Preston, USA Today best-selling author of The Mathews Family series*

~*~

"Kay's stories will make you laugh in glee and sigh with happiness."

~*Michelle C. Reilly, author of The Anathergians series*

Dedications

This book is dedicated to the daring hearts
who have taken a chance on love—
the brave souls who have stepped off a cliff
into the abyss,
and found solid ground.

~*~

Thank you to my muse.

~*~

Also, thank you to Michelle C. Reilly, Diane Deeds,
Tisha Wilson, Rebecca Andrews, Victoria Miller,
and Scott Kelley.

Chapter One

The last thing Elle needed was for Michael Williams, the businessman from New York, to freak out. At least she could call him by his first name, and hopefully that would set him at ease. The seconds flew by quickly, and she knew there was no other way around it—she had to tell him now, before he noticed on his own.

She squared her shoulders and said in a low, serious tone, "Michael, listen to me. Do not stop walking, and don't look. There's a mountain lion on the trail ahead of us."

He immediately froze in his sneakers and scanned the area ahead in a panic. Elle grabbed his sleeve and urged him along.

"Don't panic. Keep walking at a steady pace. Don't look directly at her," Elle directed. Growing up in Denver, hiking was a way of life. She was well educated about the possible dangers, and she knew how to deal with predators.

She sneaked another peek at Michael. His tall frame almost shielded her petite form from the early August sun, which made her wonder if he remembered to apply sun protection to his fair, city-boy skin. No matter. There were more pressing things to think about.

"She knows we're here. If we stop or turn around it might trigger a chase reaction. She's not aggressive, only resting."

****

Michael's heart beat forcefully against his ribs as he watched the ground, extremely careful of his footing. At least the trail was wide enough they could walk side by side. He glanced at Elle, who seemed to glide along effortlessly, her feet barely seeming to hit the ground. She was the younger sister of Randall, the man who owned Stone Mountain Partners, the advertising agency he and his uncle were currently intent on purchasing. Randall was a tall awkward man, and Michael had expected his sister to be the same. But she wasn't. She was petite, blonde, and absolutely stunning in the dappled sunlight that filtered through the trees.

Elle walked near the edge of the trail with a small drop-off to her left. He chastised himself for letting her take the dangerous side. It wasn't very gentlemanly of him. Neither was the fleeting thought that he might be able to outrun her should the cougar spring into action. He guessed she could outrun him anyway. He put his arm around her shoulder. It was a protective gesture, but also worked to steady his own body as his knees felt dangerously close to buckling.

"Michael Williams Killed by Cougar in Denver…" He imagined the headline in the Business section of the *New York Times*. Ha, as if his demise would make the news. Theirs wasn't a giant company. Steele Insights was midsize, at best. Maybe he'd get a one-sentence mention in a sidebar.

Why, again, had he decided to invite himself along on this adventure? Oh yeah, because he wanted to buy their company. If it weren't for the stubborn and mysterious silent partner who vetoed their first offer, the deal would already be sealed, and he wouldn't be facing sudden death at that very moment.

"Relax," Elle told him.

Flashing dot patterns passed in front of his eyes, and he wasn't sure if it had to do with the cat to the side of the trail in front of him or the sexy feline under his left arm. They were closing in on the big cat fast. If he was going to die, he wasn't prepared in the least. He thought of all the things he still wanted to do with his life: climb Mount Kilimanjaro, see Mount Vesuvius, scuba dive in the Great Barrier Reef, and visit the Louvre. He might never do any of it, it seemed. Not in this lifetime, anyways. If he got out of there, he'd make it a point to do one big trip a year.

"Keep talking. She's probably hoping we don't even notice her." Elle calmly interrupted his panicked thoughts.

"This is a perfectly normal thing for you, isn't it?" he asked in exasperation while licking his dry lips and trying to focus on the reason he was there—to be friendly with Randall and the rest of the team. Schmoozing wasn't his strong suit, so when he'd heard them mention they were going on a group hike, he'd chimed in with "hey, I like to hike."

He cringed. When they were driving up the mountain and Randall said his sister was joining them, Michael was sure he'd made the right choice. Stone Mountain's silent partner had to be Elle. She was Randall's sister, after all. Since their dad had been the previous owner, reason determined he had passed the business to his children.

She appeared to glance at him, but Michael couldn't really tell since her eyes were hidden behind sunglasses.

"Well, no, we don't get cougars all the time. Just be glad it's not a bear. That's much worse, especially in spring when they have cubs."

"Jesus!" He looked at her and tightened his grip slightly, feeling her body stiffen against his at the same time. He tried to swallow, but his spit was like sand.

"We're almost there. It's okay. Keep talking." She smirked, and he wasn't sure if she was making fun of him or not.

"About what?" he asked. Talking seemed an absurd and impossible suggestion, considering the danger that tracked their movements from atop a boulder about twenty feet off the path ahead of them.

"It doesn't matter. Keep your voice at a normal tone and pretend you don't notice her. What's your favorite beer?"

"Um…" Distracted by visions of headlines proclaiming a deadly animal attack, he couldn't recall a single brand name at the moment. All he could conjure were claws and teeth.

"The weather is nice today, don't you think? What a perfect August day," she said cheerfully and a little louder than needed.

He followed her cue. "Yeah, and it's definitely warmer up here than I thought. You were right. I should have brought water. Ah, a breeze would be really nice right about now." His voice cracked slightly, and as they walked under the mountain lion's rocky perch he was certain he heard a low growl of warning.

"Okay, we've passed her. But don't turn around. She's probably still watching us." Elle shrugged his arm off her shoulder.

"How do you know it was a female anyway?"

"The way she was lying there. You didn't see a penis, did you?"

"I didn't look. You told me not to."

"Yes, you did. But congratulations anyway, Michael. You kept your cool. I wonder if the others even saw her. She blended in pretty well, they may have missed her."

He laughed nervously. "I almost pissed myself."

"Good thing I didn't point out the bear a half mile back."

"Raging Bitch!"

"Excuse me?" Elle exclaimed.

"You asked my favorite beer. It's Raging Bitch from Flying Dog Brewery. I finally remembered, and I could really use one right now."

"I see." She giggled.

He wiped his brow. "Was…was there a bear? Did you say there *really* was a bear back there?" He glanced at her.

A slight smile tripped the corner of her lips. "No."

She *was* teasing him. But he didn't care at the moment. This was her element, not his. He was used to dealing with cougars of the human female variety, the type that strolled up Fifth Avenue in leopard print pants. He could handle that type of cougar—he knew their game—but he couldn't read Elle. She was a variety of female he was not familiar with. He'd never been with a woman who would be happy to be on a hike.

They strolled in silence for a few minutes to catch up with the rest of the group, who were taking a break. Each man had found a boulder to sit upon and they were all drinking water.

"So you've been to Denver before? Is that how you know the brewery?" She turned to Michael as they neared the group.

"A few times…yeah, you could say that." His smoker's lungs protested the fresh air, but he tried to control his labored breathing.

Be cool, dude.

She touched his arm. "Come over here with me. There's a great view you should see."

Michael quickly glanced over at the rest of the group. The three men—hopefully his future employees—lounged on the boulders and engaged in their own animated discussions. He turned and followed her through the trees. They emerged on another smooth rock face with a sweeping view of the valley below them and the mountains across. It reminded him of one of the framed motivational posters in the conference room back in New York, only this was the real deal. He hated those stupid posters his uncle had hung everywhere. It wasn't the messages on them that he hated, but the fact that the messages were lost on his uncle.

"Wow," was all he could muster.

"Yeah, it is beautiful. It takes my breath away every time. I come up here often, to this very spot. It's my little sanctuary." She turned, offering him the straw from her hydration pack. "Here, drink this. I noticed you didn't bring any."

The straw rested near her face so he hesitated, feeling a sudden wave of irritating pre-pubescent shyness surge through his body. She removed the clip, which stretched it an extra few inches in his direction.

"Do you want me to take off the whole pack so you can wear it, since it appears we're going to be sharing it today?"

Michael was embarrassed about neglecting to bring his own water, but he was thirsty and appreciative that she hadn't called attention to his lack of preparation in front of the other men. He leaned in to drink, and a passing breeze wafted across them, carrying her cinnamon scent. The cool water washed over his tongue and slid down his parched throat. He realized it had been a long time since he'd been that close to any woman's face besides Sandra's, and he felt the strange urge to kiss her. He noticed that she'd closed her eyes and wondered what thoughts swam through her mind.

He closed his own eyes and relished the relief the water brought.

"What were you thinking anyway, coming up here with no water?" she asked suddenly, causing him to lean back in surprise.

He wasn't sure how to respond. Before he could form any words, she disappeared through the trees to rejoin the group. He rushed to keep up.

"Hey, did you guys see that mountain lion about a quarter mile back?" she asked as they approached the group. The men sat up and all shook their heads.

"Well, perhaps you need to be a bit more observant. She was lying on a boulder a few feet up from the trail, but if one of you had tripped or made a sudden loud movement, you might have piqued her interest. So be a little more observant. Blood makes me queasy."

The men looked at Michael for confirmation, as if they didn't want to take the scolding from Elle. "Yeah, she was a big one. Plus, there was a bear back near the beginning of the trail, too, but it was farther off the path. So take her advice and keep your eyes open."

****

Elle straggled behind with Michael for the rest of the hike, rationing her water and sharing an energy bar. The rest of the group quickly outdistanced them again. She hoped they weren't bored waiting in the parking lot, but she was sure they were only about ten minutes behind them.

As a matter of fact, she kind of liked hanging back with Michael. Sure, Randall hadn't been entirely up front with her about the situation today. She was certain Randall felt the lasers she shot at him from her eyes when she'd realized he'd brought the investor along without giving her a heads-up. Of course, if he had told her, she wouldn't have come, and would have missed out on a nice hike. Plus, she had to appreciate the thought Randall had put into it.

"Let's see how he does on our turf, and then we can see if we can trust him with Stone," he'd said.

Yeah, he was right, they needed to know him better before they entrusted him with their company.

She'd appreciated the way Michael backed her up with the group when she scolded them to pay better attention to their surroundings when they were hiking. He'd even added the part about the bear, which she knew was only for her benefit.

"Do you know Randall's partner?" Michael asked, abruptly breaking the silence.

Elle removed her ponytail holder and ran her hands through her hair before retying it. She tried to think of the best way to answer his question without raising suspicions.

"Mmm," she answered, which wasn't really a yes or a no. *God, that was dumb.*

"No one seems to know how I can get in touch with him. No one besides Randall, and he isn't budging. I'd really like the opportunity to talk to him in person if you could arrange it."

"I think he's out of the country right now. What did you need to talk to him about?" She glanced at him, squinting against the sun.

"Obviously, Randall's told you we're in talks to buy the company, right?"

She nodded.

"Well, I can't seem to get his partner to agree on anything. I send paperwork, and he sends it back. I would appreciate some insight on him. I'm just at a loss." He ran his hand through his hair, and strands stuck straight up. "Randall seems comfortable with the price. I mean, why else would I be here hiking with you all?" He glanced down at her for a moment. "Ah, never mind. Forget it. I really shouldn't be boring you with this nonsense, especially since you saved my life and all back there. It must be the altitude."

Elle opened her mouth to question him, but he broke in first.

"Back there with the mountain lion. I would have been in the headlines if you weren't there to hold me up. I wouldn't have known what to do. I would have ran away and probably been torn to shreds. So thank you. Truly."

For a moment, Elle thought she saw a flicker of vulnerability in his eyes, and something else she couldn't identify. "You're welcome." She smiled. The cat was resting and had a visibly full belly. There was no way she would have attacked them, unless they'd been dumb enough to either approach her directly or run away. But she'd let Michael continue to think he'd actually been in very grave danger. It was prudent to let him feel like he owed her one. It was also prudent to allow him to continue thinking the silent partner was a man.

She offered him the straw of the hydration pack again. He leaned in to drink, and she felt guilty for playing the little game of cat and mouse with him, even though she and Randall had agreed to it. Now that Michael was in front of her, it seemed more real, and she felt like she was in high school again. That awkwardness had less to do with the hot guy standing in front of her than with the fact she'd let Randall corral her into a dumb stunt again.

Hot? Yes, he was hot. But he'd be more her type if he hadn't seemed so out of his element. She preferred a more rugged man, like the Marlboro men of old print ads. But Michael did have edginess to him, a sexiness that she couldn't pinpoint. She liked him in the jeans, T-shirt and tennis shoes he was wearing that day, but knew that wasn't his usual attire. He was a businessman from New York, and although men in suits usually appealed to most women, they didn't appeal to her. Sitting on the board of her birth parent's company had put her in contact with suits before, and she found them to be stiff, humorless, and unapproachable. And if they were that way in San Diego, she could imagine how they were in New York, a city built around suits.

Her adoptive family needed the extra cash that selling the business would provide, even if she didn't.

Elle had enough—she'd always have enough, thankfully—since her birth parents had set up her trust fund even when she was an infant. But her adoptive family, especially her dad, didn't like accepting her charity and she had to respect the booger for it.

She and Michael rounded one of the last curves on the hiking trail.

"Hey, are there other companies you are looking at buying?" Elle asked, stopping to face Michael on the path.

"My company? Yes. That's what we do at Steele Insights. Myself? No. Stone Mountain Partners is my current focus. At the moment, no, I'm not looking elsewhere, and I would like the chance to explain my plan to Randall's partner in person before we decide to move on. I'm certain I could persuade him. We have an excellent track record as our website showcases."

He glanced at her lips, so she moistened them with her tongue before speaking. It was an innocent gesture, yet calculated. She knew how to play a man and it came in handy in the boardroom sometimes. "I looked at your website, but my own research shows you often sell the companies for a profit to a competitor a year or so later, and most of the employees end up being laid off in the process."

"I see you've done your homework. Yes, that does happen from time to time, but sometimes it's the best thing."

"Laying people off is a good thing?"

"It's a matter of perspective. Most of them end up being rehired by the new companies we form."

"...and lose their seniority and vacation time. Et cetera. Right?"

"Not necessarily. You seem personally invested in this. Are you the silent partner?" He stopped on the path, looking directly into her sunglass-covered eyes.

"Me? No." Elle laughed. "God, no. I've just taken a few business classes."

"I see."

She turned and continued walking. "Come on then, let's get out of here. We shouldn't keep the others waiting too long."

Chapter Two

Monday morning couldn't creep by any slower. Michael hated working with numbers and details. They made his head spin. On more than one occasion he had requested not to be the one to do the acquisition house calls, but his uncle, John Steele, had insisted that Michael was the ideal man for the job.

"With your good looks and charm, you could sell oceanfront property in Denver," John had assured him. "Besides, you're better at math than you think."

Michael knew his uncle was right. He was good at math, but he still hated it.

This particular acquisition, however, did seem to have its perks. First of all, the owner had a cute sister who had featured prominently in his imagination since the hike on Saturday. Second, he was offered the use of Stone Mountain's small conference room as a temporary office during the acquisition talks, which beat the hell out of working from his hotel room when he was in town. At least he got to be around other people. Plus, it gave him the positive vibe that, although he had already made them a very generous offer, they might well be ready to sign off on the deal for a few thousand dollars more. Why else would they have been so kind?

Whenever he traversed the halls, he was able to interact with the employees on a friendly basis, and it seemed as if they were rather good-natured and open to his presence there. He was glad of it, too. He had been on acquisitions before when the employees were suspicious and bitter, and that could really throw a curveball into things. But it seemed Randall was a great manager, as his employees trusted him enough to allow a stranger into their building without giving him the evil eye.

He only wished that he could move the acquisition along a bit faster. Unfortunately, there was one thing that was causing the backup—the silent partner.

After their conversation on the hike, Michael was almost certain that Elle was Randall's silent partner; although, he couldn't quite fathom why she and her brother were trying to hide it. Of course they wanted more money, but that could have been discussed in face-to-face negotiations.

Michael was intrigued by how little he really knew about Elle. He had nothing to base his assumptions on, having already searched the Internet for any information on Elle Johnston, and came up with zilch other than a social networking site that was set to private mode. Her pictures on the site were nothing compared to flesh and blood.

He let out a long, steady breath and pushed his chair back from the conference table. He decided it would be better not to share his theory about Elle with his uncle, and he reminded himself that his sleuthing skills had failed him recently when he'd discovered his fiancée—or ex-fiancée—in his bed with their realtor. He hadn't seen that coming at all, but in hindsight, the clues were blatant.

The wall clock showed it was a quarter until noon,

and time for his second cup of coffee and third cigarette of the day. Yes, he kept count. It was that math thing again.

He dropped his eyes to the floor as he made his way from the conference room to the break room, hoping that no one would notice the ridiculously bright raccoon-mask-shaped sunburn he sported across his face. After successfully navigating the halls, he relaxed in the break room, letting his guard down briefly as he poured a cup to bring outside with him.

"How are you feeling today?" a familiar voice asked behind him. He didn't have to turn to know who it was, but he turned anyway, temporarily forgetting about his sunburn until he saw the shocked expression on her face.

"Whoa! No sunblock either? I had some, you could have asked," she said. "That'll peel for sure."

Blue! Brilliant, shimmering blue eyes. He hadn't seen her eyes during their hike, as they'd been hidden behind sunglasses the whole time, and he'd always been a sucker for blue eyes. She wore jeweled sandals, torn jeans and a lime green, long-sleeved shirt with a misshapen Buddha on it, protruding outward over her breasts. Her warm blonde hair hung long, loose, and wavy as she leaned casually against the doorframe.

"I see you've already made yourself quite at home here," she said. "Randall told me he let you use the conference room."

"What are you doing here?" he asked, in a tone that sounded a bit too firm.

"Oh, no 'how are you' or 'nice to see you'?" She tilted her head to the side, causing a loose curl to graze her breast.

He turned back to the coffee, adding cream and stirring absently. "I didn't mean to sound rude. You just surprised me."

She laughed and shrugged. "I was in the neighborhood and stopped by to say hi to Randall. He mentioned you were going to Hamada's for sushi today."

He turned around, leaning against the counter. "Yeah, I've heard great things about it. Will you be joining us?"

"I'd love to, but actually, I have to run. It was good to see you. I'm sure I'll see you again soon." She waved and turned.

"Likewise."

He'd truly hoped she was going to join them for lunch, but it was probably best if she didn't. His mind needed to be clear.

Later that night, Michael flew the red-eye back to New York for a few days, the same as he had the past two weeks, to check in at home and at the office. During the flight, he fell asleep and had an absurd dream that the mountain lion they encountered on the path had spoken aloud to him in Elle's voice.

"I could eat you alive, you little raccoon," it had said. The lion produced a pair of chopsticks and pounced on him, while a nude Elle lounged lazily nearby on a fallen tree like a wood nymph, seemingly uninterested in his plight.

He woke with a start to the stewardess asking if he wanted something to drink.

"No, thanks," he said, and then settled back in the leather seat, staring out the window into dark oblivion and trying to refocus his thoughts on the mess he had yet to sort out at home. Between mountain lions, sunburns, dehydration, and a silent partner that gave new meaning to the word "silent," he looked forward to returning to New York, where the only cougars he had to worry about were on Fifth Avenue, and the only bears were on Wall Street. It was easy to be anonymous and avoid conversations in the city, and he relished it occasionally.

****

Michael surveyed the impeccably dressed restaurant patrons, who smiled pleasantly and benignly back at him as he sliced into his medium-rare filet mignon. A young man played the piano in the corner, and the gentle clinking of utensils and hushed conversations surrounded him. He took a generous sip of Cabernet Sauvignon, the perfect pairing to his meal.

Still, if it were up to him, he would have ordered Chinese at home and sorted through e-mails. But Uncle John insisted they meet for dinner to discuss the negotiations in Denver. Specifically, he wanted to discuss the problems with the silent partner.

True to form, John Steele was already half an hour late, probably due to a visit with his regular call girl, which left Michael sitting at the restaurant alone for far too long. He decided to make the best of it, ordered dinner and his favorite wine, and planned on downing the entire bottle himself before his uncle showed up, if he showed up at all.

If the other patrons knew what he'd been through the past month, perhaps they would have raised their glasses to him instead of raising their eyebrows at a man dining alone with a bottle of wine.

Michael had grabbed a cab from the airport to take

him to the condo he shared with Sandra, his fiancée. He had come home early in hopes of surprising her and picked up the mail on the way in. But when he laid it on the counter he had seen an unfamiliar set of keys. More than that, he saw the remnants of a homemade pasta dinner for two on the table and realized that the sounds he heard weren't coming from their porn-addicted neighbor's TV, but from his bedroom.

Michael took another long drink of wine, and a waiter appeared almost instantly to refill the glass. As well he should have, considering what the bottle had cost.

He trekked down the hall and thrown the bedroom door open with gusto. In the darkness he made out two pale, naked bodies suddenly separating, so he threw the switch for the overhead ceiling fan, a light he never used because it was way too bright.

"Michael, let me explain..." Sandra started, while Mark muttered expletives and pulled on his clothes. The overhead light was glaring.

"Get the hell out of my apartment! Both of you!" he exclaimed, the sight making him feel more vindicated than hurt.

"But...but," Sandra whined, still clutching the sheet to her chest.

"But...I don't give a shit, get the fuck out of here. Now!"

She obliged.

As soon as they left, Michael went out in search of a store that sold new locks, which was surprisingly easy to find. Apparently, people changed their locks pretty often in his neighborhood. When he returned, he changed the locks then fell into a fitful sleep on the sofa.

"Ah, there you are, Michael," John said, as his large form settled into the chair opposite him. The waiter appeared again and poured a glass of wine for John, emptying the bottle.

The waiter turned his attention on Michael. "Would you like another one, sir?"

"Yes, please."

Michael wasn't surprised at all that John didn't apologize for being late. He didn't even seem to notice.

"What are you eating there, sport?" John nodded at Michael's half-empty plate.

"The filet, of course."

"Hmm, predictable." John opened his menu.

"It's the best," Michael replied irritably.

"Yeah, yeah, so what's the news in Denver?" John asked, not looking up from his menu.

"Well, the partner is out of the country. So I don't know if that means he's a foreign investor, or what. I don't know what to think. They've let me use their conference room, which tells me they are warming up to the idea, but I haven't heard a peep from the other guy. Zilch."

"Do you know his name yet?"

"Nope. Sorry, Uncle, but Randall let it slip that he was foreign," he lied, consciously leaving Elle out of the equation. If John knew what he suspected, he would launch a full-scale background check on her, digging up who knows what and completely invading her privacy. John knew no boundaries, but Michael did, and information freely listed on the Internet was as far as he would go.

"So offer them a few thousand more. See what that

does."

"A few thousand? I don't see how that will increase our bargaining power any. We've already offered them full current net worth as it is. I think we should offer them at least a hundred thousand more, based on their current contracts. Also, it seems that Randall wants an agreement that we will keep the current staff."

John shrugged. "Maybe he wants a new car out of it. A golden parachute and all that. You know the type. We can discuss the final offer tomorrow at the office. As far as the staff, go ahead and agree to it. Write something up, but keep the wording vague and open to interpretation. When we sell them, it won't matter anyway."

Michael hated knowing John already had plans to sell Stone Mountain Partners for a profit almost immediately after the acquisition. All the kind negotiations regarding staff and benefits were purely for show. It felt so dirty, and they had done it many times before.

The waiter brought another bottle of wine and politely took John's order.

"How's it going with that woman of yours? Sarah? Sammy?"

"It's Sandra. And, we're not together anymore. She moved out."

"Really? What did you do this time? She really was a nice woman, you know. A good woman," John said, shaking his head.

"Oh, I don't know. Maybe I was afraid of commitment." Michael didn't feel the need to divulge any other information to his crass uncle.

John laughed. "Hell, yeah, aren't we all? It's a scary thought to imagine parking your car in the same garage for the rest of your life, know what I mean? Besides, I know a few great girls if you're looking for some fun to tide you over. No commitments."

"Uh, thanks. I'll keep that in mind." He most definitely planned to forget that invitation as soon as he could. Everyone at the firm knew John spent time—and lots of money—on call girls, and it was getting way out of hand. Michael was afraid that any day a major investor might find out and back out of a deal. Then what would happen? All hell would break loose, that's what, and it would be a major embarrassment.

Michael felt helpless, though. What could he do about it? Try to talk to his uncle? There was no talking to him, he'd tried to before. John didn't see the big deal in "letting off a little steam on the weekends," as he'd put it.

Fine—what John did on the weekends was his business, but what he decided to do on company time belonged to and was the ultimate responsibility of the company. They were publically traded, after all. John was the CEO, but Michael was the majority stock holder. He held a conservative amount in his name, and a larger account in his mother's name. If the need ever arose, he could certainly have her transfer her shares to him. Knowing that fact helped Michael sleep a bit better each night.

Plus, he was pretty certain it had never crossed his uncle's wayward mind.

****

It drizzled in New York, and the city lights reflected like multicolored jewels on the pavement during the cab ride back to Queens. Michael appreciated small glimpses of beauty in the city. The clean smell of rain reminded him that the mountain-surrounded city he'd grown up in was far more natural than the steel skyscrapers surrounding him in this one.

But he still loved New York. It was vibrant, ever-changing, and inspiring. There was always a new show to see, a new exhibit to visit, or some trendy new restaurant to try. No wonder people tended to move there in their youth, chasing dreams. He'd once heard someone say that everyone should live in New York for a year, and he believed they were right.

That night, as Michael lay on the sofa, he stared at the slow moving ceiling fan blades and listened to the rhythmic sound of the air cutting in their wake. *Whoosh, whoosh, whoosh.*

He couldn't pinpoint the exact moment when his relationship with Sandra had gone *whoosh*. He once thought he had loved her, and that he'd been happy. But now that she was gone, he was almost surprised to find he didn't really miss her at all. The only thing he really missed was his bed, as he had been unable to sleep in it since that night. He planned to buy a new one, but hadn't accomplished that task yet.

Truth be told, he missed her lasagna, too, but he could live without it. Besides, he'd already found a suitable substitute at a nearby Italian restaurant.

Unable to sleep, he stood up and lit a cigarette. Leaning against the sofa, he stared back at his own reflection in the window, shirtless and in white boxers. He walked toward his reflection and turned from side to side, observing with dismay that he appeared to have gained a couple of extra pounds over the last few months, no doubt the result of all the extra time spent sitting at a computer focused on expanding the business. Nothing a few weeks at the gym can't fix, he thought as he patted his sides. He walked over to the wet bar, flipped a low light on and studied the mirror on the wall. On his face he saw the telltale tan lines of the day hiking in the sun with no sunblock, and his nose had started to peel.

Michael looked back and scrutinized his designer living room set. Seized by a sudden thought, he reached down and pulled the cushions off the bottom half of the sofa. Indeed, it was a sofa bed. Still feeling the wine, he did a small touchdown dance and proceeded to pull out the bed portion. He laughed aloud at himself, having never thought to pull the bed out before. He settled onto the mattress and stretched out triumphantly, placing his hands behind his head.

Sometimes small victories held as much satisfaction as big ones.

Late the next evening, Michael was set to take the red-eye into Denver for the weekend again. He double-checked to make sure he had everything he needed for the next four days packed in his ever-ready suitcase, then placed it by the front door.

He still had twenty minutes until the town car was supposed to show up, so he sat down on his couch to have a cigarette. The last time he had seen Sandra, the morning after she'd left, made him uncomfortable. As pissed and angry as he was, he hated leaving it that way and felt unsettled since it happened.

He woke with a pounding headache, but quickly realized the pounding was coming from the front door, not his head. He stood a bit too quickly and felt dizzy as he made his way to the door. He was still dressed in the same rumpled clothes from the day before. He looked through the peephole and saw Sandra standing with her arms crossed and a weasly looking Mark Janis, the realtor, behind her.

Oh, this ought to be good, he thought, then opened the door and stood with his hands on his hips.

Sandra tossed her arms in the air, exasperated. "Well..."

He nonchalantly shrugged his shoulders and narrowed his eyes at the man behind her who averted his gaze to the floor. "Well what?"

"So, this is it, then?" she asked.

"Yeah, I suppose it is."

She nodded, her jaw rigid. She looked past him. "What about my stuff?"

"I'll have it delivered to Mark's place," he said, barely withholding the snicker that formed in his throat when he saw her face.

"You asshole!" Sandra glared at both of them then turned and stormed off.

Mark lowered his head and followed her like a trained poodle.

"Congratulations, you're the perfect couple!" Michael called after them before shutting the door.

It had been childish of him to add the insult, but at the time it seemed appropriate. Now, he thought better of it. He knew he hadn't loved her, and guessed she had sensed it as well and looked elsewhere. Life waits for no one.

Yet, he didn't feel a pressing need to call her and apologize, though. He'd just let it be a lesson in remaining more mindful in the future. If he sensed uneasiness in a relationship, he decided he'd tackle it head-on instead of letting it fester in the background. No more wasted time. It was fun to fantasize about do overs, but not realistic.

He heard a horn beep on the street downstairs and knew it was the town car, so he grabbed his suitcase and locked up. He relaxed in the back seat on the way to JFK.

Chapter Three

Elle watched Michael shuffle from one foot to another while leaning against the counter in the lobby of the barbeque restaurant. She usually went for the more rugged type, but there was still something about him that intrigued her, despite the fact she wanted to shove his most recent offer up his ass.

No, his nose—rather, his red, peeling nose. Better to leave his nicely rounded ass out of the equation as it might throw her thinking askew.

She cleared her throat as the seconds ticked by, and eyed him up and down as he had done to her only moments before. He wore black dress shoes, gray slacks, and a monogrammed white dress shirt, rolled up at the sleeves, and a silver watch. Her gaze lingered here and there as she sized him up and formed an opinion.

Michael Williams was a soft city boy, and she was willing to bet he not only indulged in regular manicures but perhaps even enjoyed the occasional facial. She wondered whether he had rolled up his sleeves for fear of getting his expensive white designer dress shirt dirty with barbecue sauce. He probably wore designer underwear as well.

Boxers or briefs? Her gaze traveled south. *Briefs, probably. Expensive white designer briefs. Tighty whities.*

He was definitely not her type.

She smirked as her gaze traveled back up to his eyes. They were staring back into hers.

Caught red-handed. Her smirk faded and her cheeks reddened. She grabbed at a strand of hair to twirl in her fingers and pretended to be interested in a framed painting of a pig in an apron that was hung behind his left shoulder.

Something primal lurked below the surface of his gaze, and it drew her back in. It was as if she stared into the eyes of a caged animal set to pounce. Not one that had been born in a zoo, but one that had been captured in the wild and placed in captivity. Perhaps he hadn't always been a city boy...

He blinked and the spell was broken. Reality set in, and she looked away with a quiet sigh.

Very few people in Denver knew the Johnstons adopted Elle when she was a child. Thus, even fewer people knew she sat on the board of her birth parent's land development company in San Diego, Duncan Land Development. She received generous compensation for it, and was listed as Gabrielle Duncan on their website, in keeping with the family name.

However, if someone were to dig into the company's SEC filings, they'd find Gabrielle Johnston on the list, but no one would ever have a reason to do that. It wasn't like she was purposefully hiding it; it just worked out that way.

When Jake got sick and signed the company over to them early that spring, they chose to keep the deal silent. Jake reasoned that it was no one's business but theirs. Even the employees weren't aware Jake was no longer the owner. They'd had suspicions, of course, as soon as Michael had shown up. Randall had assured his staff that even though they were looking at an acquisition offer, the employees' well-being was of paramount importance to him.

After Michael initially contacted Stone Mountain Partners, the siblings were intrigued by the idea and decided their silent partnership would be an advantage in negotiations. Randall and Elle thought it wise to put off Michael's offer for a week or two at least, and drive up the price. Randall decided he would do the negotiating and she would wait in the background until it was time to pounce.

But as Elle followed the waitress to their booth, feeling Michael's gaze on her as she walked, their charade seemed to be growing bigger and messier than any other trouble Randall had ever convinced her to get into. Now, here she was having a friendly barbeque lunch with both of them.

****

Michael absently tapped his foot on the wooden floor under the table and tried to ignore the fact that Elle's denim dress hugged the curves of her body as if it were tailored only for her. It wasn't that it was tight or low-cut. It was a modest dress, but on her it was incredibly sexy. He imagined the rough denim fabric caressing her skin underneath before clearing his throat and turning his attention to Randall, who blathered about the Broncos.

Watching football was a luxury for men with time on their hands. Michael didn't have time on his hands, and hadn't for over a year. But he kept up on sports information because he knew it was good conversational material and a way for men to bond. It was a very logical way to look at it, and he could throw out a few statistics here and there and an instant camaraderie would form, which could be excellent for business. He interjected a few thoughts on the Bronco's upcoming season, sending Randall into a diatribe over their defense strategies from the previous year, and how he hoped they'd improve.

Michael nodded and looked at Elle, who appeared completely uninterested. She was watching the trivia game on a TV set in the bar. He caught her eye and she smiled.

The siblings really looked nothing alike. Elle was petite and beautiful, with an oval face and graceful limbs, while Randall was tall, angular, and gawky. Michael wondered if Elle was wearing a red silk slip beneath her denim dress, or perhaps a lace bra and thong. Maybe she wasn't wearing anything at all.

He squeezed lemon into his iced tea and a squirt of juice shot in Elle's direction, which she thankfully didn't seem to notice.

"Has anyone ever told you two that you don't look anything alike?" he asked the siblings during a lull in football-related conversation.

"Well, that's because she's adopted," Randall said matter-of-factly, and closed his menu.

"Oh?" He wasn't sure if Randall meant it as a joke or if he was serious.

"Yeah. I feel bad for her, really," Randall went on, "seeing how I'm the one with the good-looking genes and all. It was really rough for her in high school. All of her friends wanted to date me. It was embarrassing. She didn't get any dates."

"Oh, come on. You're full of it." Elle smiled over

her sweet tea and shook her head, suppressing a laugh.

Randall chuckled. "So a few of us guys might go hiking again this weekend. You in again, Ellie?" he asked. "Actually, you're invited, too, Michael. There's a lodge we're going to have dinner at afterward. I could pick you up in the morning."

"Are you going this time?" Michael asked Elle directly.

"I don't think I can," she answered. "I have some…research to do. I'm taking some classes right now, but I might be able to meet up with everyone afterward."

"What are you studying?" Michael asked, leaning forward.

"Anthropology."

"Ah." He took a long, thoughtful sip from his tea. Anthropology, a subject he knew little to nothing about. He then reminded himself that Elle was a subject he knew little to nothing about, having neglected to ask her any polite questions the previous weekend. *What do you do for a living? Are you single? Do you sleep naked?*

"Is that your major?" asked Michael.

"Well, I already have a bachelor's in art history. I'm just taking these for fun. It's fascinating stuff."

"So what do you do?"

"This and that. I volunteer a lot. Actually, I'm between jobs at the moment." She gave a pleasant smile and, somewhat nervously, twirled a strand of hair with her finger.

Michael was about to ask her what she used to do but their food arrived. Besides, she didn't seem particularly talkative. He decided to assume she was single, since no mention of a significant other had been made in the past two weeks, and there wasn't a ring on her finger. He hadn't found anything indicating a marriage on the Internet, but he hadn't used any paid sites.

****

Elle certainly did not appreciate her brother getting all chummy with Michael. What was he thinking? It was Randall's big, risky idea to play this charade game, but the signals he was sending were too mixed. Michael was sure to be interpreting them as a green light that all was good, and the acquisition was a green light.

Of course he'd go to lunch with them. Of course he'd go on the hike with them. Why wouldn't he? He wanted to buy them. He wanted them to feel comfortable with him.

She pinched her brother's thigh hard under the table and hoped he'd gotten the point. The dummy. It seemed Randall was trying to play cupid with her and Michael, which was an even dumber idea than the charade had been. She knew he wanted her to start dating again. Heck, everyone did, but good grief…she couldn't date the man that wanted to buy their company.

Michael excused himself from the table and headed toward the restroom.

In his absence, she turned to her brother. "In the history of bad ideas, this is the worst idea you've ever had."

"I beg your pardon?" he asked innocently.

"You know exactly what you're doing. Setting me up with him."

"I am doing nothing of the sort." He wiped his

31

mouth with a napkin.

"Oh, really?"

"And, what about you? I saw you eyeing him in the lobby."

"I did not." She looked away.

"Yes, you most certainly did. I think everyone saw. It was almost pornographic. Admit it, sister." Randall shrugged. "He's a good-looking guy, there's nothing wrong with it."

Before she could respond, Michael returned to the table. She studied him. Should she go on another hike with him? No, she couldn't do it. Not that he was bad company because, truth be told, he wasn't, but she'd already planned to spend the afternoon with their dad at the hospital, as she usually did while he received his chemotherapy treatment. It was their time to talk and play cards.

Besides, there was no sense in cultivating a crush on someone that didn't live within driving distance. New York was how many miles away—a thousand? More?

Heck, why was she even pondering the distance? It was too far.

Then again New York was a wonderful town, and she very much enjoyed the trips she'd taken there.

She was glad to get out of the hike, and she struggled valiantly to convince herself.

Chapter Four

Elle made love to Michael. Her warm bare skin smelled of cinnamon and pine, and her breath came in raspy gasps near his ear. She straddled him, grinding her hips roughly against his. Her hair was wild in the glow of the light shining through the slit in the curtains of the motel room. He cupped her bare breasts in his palms. This was raw, pure sex.

"Holy hell, babe," he growled, pulling her back down to kiss her.

Elle's hand flailed against the clock radio on the hotel nightstand, turning it on. Michael groped in the darkness to shut it off, but he hit the light switch instead. And the bed was empty.

"Fuck," he mumbled. "Fucking dream."

The hotel phone was ringing. He shook his head and reached for it.

"Hello?" he answered, his voice raspy.

"Good morning Mr. Williams, this is your six a.m. wake up call," said a male voice before the line went dead.

"Uh, thanks," grumbled Michael and hung up the phone and lay back on the bed, his erection throbbing against the sheet. He rubbed his hands through his hair and over his face before glancing again at the clock.

Randall was going to be picking him up in a half hour so they could meet the rest of the guys for breakfast before the hike. There was no time to go back to sleep and finish his dream, as he longed to, so he settled for a quick self-pleasuring session instead. He hadn't felt like doing that in a very long time and although it brought some relief, it wasn't enough.

Afterward, Michael eased into a nice warm shower and focused his thoughts on Stone Mountain Partners—or SMP, as Elle had called it. He was convinced Elle was SMP's silent partner, and she and her brother were attempting to pull off some sort of charade to drive the price up. Seriously, did they really think him a fool? But he would play along. Why not? After all, she was very cute, but he was also glad to have a reason to be back in Denver for a while, and he had to admit he was starting to really question the way his uncle liked to do business. Buying small, successful mom-and-pop companies, selling them to larger companies, and then casting their loyal, long-time employees to the winds weren't actions that set well with him.

But then again, he was just the math guy.

Yet, the math guy owned the majority share of stock and if the need arose to assert that power, he would.

****

Elle woke before the sun that morning and hadn't been able to go back to sleep. She knew she could still change her mind and go on the hike, if she wanted to. The sun edged closer to the horizon in the window behind her, and the window for her to change her mind was fading.

If Michael hadn't already guessed that she was the silent partner, how much longer would it take for him to do the math? He'd outright asked her on the hike.

Surely he would figure it out soon, but if not, she would tell him. No more dumb games. Tonight, after dinner at the Lodge, she would tell him and be done with it.

As she sat on her bed, pulling her boots on, she smiled at the framed photo of her birth parents on her nightstand. They were both so lovely, and young, in the photo, standing on the edge of the Grand Canyon.

Elle had hiked across the Grand Canyon with Ron, her late husband, and during their visit, she'd located the exact spot her parents stood for the picture, near the El Tovar Hotel. It was important to her to have a photo with Ron there, too, so they'd grabbed a passing tourist and asked for a quick picture. That photo was displayed on her fridge under a magnet of San Diego, the town her birth parents were from.

Sometimes things happen exactly as they should.

Elle dressed and went for a brisk jog and then showered before heading over to the Johnstons. She didn't mind taking Jake to his sessions. The fatigue of caring for Jake showed on Patty's face, no matter how she tried to hide it and Elle was glad to give her a few hours rest whenever she could. Besides, she relished the precious time with her adoptive father.

The traffic moved easily that morning, and the waiting room was surprisingly empty, but she reminded herself it was Saturday and not his usual Friday appointment. Elle often wondered why that was, figuring that Saturdays would be the busier day.

"Mr. Thompson, are you ready?" asked the nurse, opening the door.

Jake glanced at Elle. "I guess it's time to get stuck again," he murmured.

"I know, Dad. I'll sit with you the whole time."

The nurse helped him down the hall to the chemotherapy room; a room Elle had spent far too much time in when Ron had been sick. She and Jake usually played cards to pass the time during his sessions, but today he had more important things on his mind.

"So Randall told me you rejected their second offer."

Elle took a breath. "I did. I sent it back, just like the first. Randall and I discussed it at length, of course. He said he talked to you."

"He did, but I want to hear your take on it."

Jake winced as the nurse attached the IV to his port.

Elle caressed his hand to soothe him as the therapy began. "I should have called you first before sending it back. What do you think, Dad, do you think they're being fair with their offer?"

Jake took a breath. "Well, you know this is hard for me. Stone Mountain is my baby. But who would have thought twenty years ago that a New York company would want to buy my little ad agency? And for one-point-two million dollars? It's humbling. But I have to think about the employees. They are what make the company, not the four walls. Many of them have been with us for a very long time. And I have to think about our customer's contracts. They might not be comfortable with new management, if it came to that, and I'd hate to make the customers uncomfortable."

A nurse walked over and adjusted the drip line.

"I don't think the customers would necessarily be uncomfortable," Elle said. "I think being attached to a national, more recognizable name would instill more confidence in our product. In the end, I think we'll keep the same long-term customers and pick up a slew of new ones. But I agree about the employees. That's why I didn't want to agree to their terms yet. I'd like them to lay out a plan for the employees first."

Jake rubbed his chin and pursed his lips. He nodded. "I agree. That's a fresh way of looking at it. And, that's exactly what we need, you know that. Fresh eyes. A shot in the arm and all that. You've only confirmed what I've been thinking."

"So you are saying you're okay with the deal for one-point-two million?"

Jake smiled. "I'm quite happy with it, as long as they include the bit about keeping the employees and upholding the current contracts. But it's ultimately up to you and Randall now." He squeezed her hand. "I wish your mom and dad could see the beautiful, smart woman you've become. It's been an honor to raise you."

"Dad..." Elle whispered, tears welling.

"No, I mean it, honey. Will and Audrey were good people; we were blessed to have them as such close friends."

There was really no question that Audrey and William Duncan's three-year-old daughter, Gabrielle, would be adopted by their close friends, Jake and Patty Johnston after their fatal car accident. William had been a land developer in San Diego, where he and Jake had grown up together. When the official adoption finally went through a year later, Jake moved the family to Denver to start an advertising agency.

"So, any new men in your life?" Jake asked, a hopeful tone lining his voice.

Michael immediately came to mind, but she pushed him out. Why had he even popped in? "No, and I'm not looking."

"Ron was a good guy, he'll be hard to replace," Jake agreed. "Even with the hair…"

"Dad…" Elle snickered.

Jake and Patty raised Elle as their own daughter and schooled her in money management, knowing that the Duncan Family Trust would be handed over to her when she turned twenty-one. On that fateful trip to San Diego to sign the trust papers, a starry eyed twenty-one-year-old Elle had met a long-haired surfer named Ron, who would be her husband less than a year later.

"He turned out okay." Jake smiled.

Initially, Jake wasn't sure what to make of Ron and his dreadlocks, but after getting to know him, he welcomed him into the family with open arms. After a short long-distance relationship, Ron moved to Denver with her and became a white water rafting guide.

When the session was over, Elle wheeled Jake out to her Jeep and helped buckle him in. She hated how weak the chemotherapy made him, but knew it was a necessary evil. The chemotherapy killed the good cells along with the bad, so only good cells would regrow. Nevertheless, it took a major toll on his body.

She drove him home, and as Patty helped him into the house, Elle went upstairs to use the restroom. After checking her appearance in the mirror and adjusting her makeup, she ran her fingers through her hair. She went back downstairs, exchanged quick kisses and said good-bye.

She got back into her Jeep, headed to the interstate, and promptly came to a complete halt.

The traffic jam ahead was truly epic in scope. Elle glanced at the dash clock, then again at the gridlock in front of her and lost all hope of making it to the Lodge on time. Also, she had absolutely no way to contact Randall as his cell phone had gone for an accidental swim in the toilet the previous week, thanks to her nephew. Randall had joked that he now had a good excuse not to have to handle any sudden calamities that might pop up at work for at least a little while until he replaced the phone.

By the time the jam loosened and she was on her way again, Elle had lost an hour in gridlock. She turned the volume up on her stereo as she drove. As she pulled into the Lodge's parking lot, she switched the blaring music off and perceived the outline of a figure near the corner of the building. Even before her headlights swept over him as she parked, she knew it was Michael. His back was still turned, and smoke rose from his fingers as she walked toward him.

"Hi, Michael," she said.

He coughed a few times before turning to face her.

"Hi, Elle," he replied, and hurriedly scuffed the cigarette beneath his foot.

Elle wore a cut-off denim skirt that grazed her tanned legs above dark brown, suede, cowboy boots, a white knit top, and she carried a light purple sweater draped over her arm. Her hair was loose and wavy again, but held back with two silver barrettes near her left ear.

"The traffic was really bad. There must have been an accident or something," she said. "I almost gave up and turned around. I hope everyone's still here."

It took him a moment to find his speech. "Yeah,

yeah, they're all here."

"How was the hike?"

"Great," he said, lamely. "At least I was more prepared this time, thanks to your pointers. We've all finished eating, but I would be happy to buy you dinner."

"That would be awesome, thank you. I'm starving."

He leaned down to pick up the cigarette butt and tossed it in a nearby ashtray. "I've been meaning to quit. I haven't always been a smoker. Gross habit."

"Good luck with that." She wondered why he'd explained that he hadn't always been a smoker. Was he trying to impress her?

He gestured for her to walk ahead and opened the door for her.

Elle received a warm reception at the table and slid into an empty chair beside Randall. Upon noticing there was already a glass of water there, she glanced sharply at Michael, but before she could say anything he picked up the glass.

"That's okay, stay there. I'll grab another chair," he said. He secured a place at the end of the long table, some distance away from her. Elle ordered a cheeseburger with mushrooms, no onions, and a light beer. Randall picked her fries off her plate when she was done. She began to wonder whether she had ketchup on her face because she noticed Michael watching her. She dabbed her lips more than she normally would, just in case. Elle tried to interest herself in the conversations around her, but it seemed to her as if she and Michael were the only ones in the room, having an inaudible conversation.

Eventually the room began to clear, and the remaining four patrons decided to move to sofas and chairs near one of the fireplaces blazing in the Lodge's lobby. Elle sat on a couch with Randall on one side and Tom, who worked as a billboard installer for their company, on the other. She stretched her tanned legs onto the ottoman in front of the couch and raised her beer toward the fire.

After relaxing for a while, Michael rose from his armchair and stepped outside for another cigarette. Tom wandered off to the bathroom, leaving Elle alone with her brother for a moment.

"Are you okay?" asked Randall quietly.

"Yes, but I'm tired. I was with Dad today, while he got his chemo."

Randall narrowed his eyes at her. "Don't go wearing yourself out."

"I told you I'm fine," she assured him. "But I appreciate your concern. I've only had two small beers."

"Still, you better let me drive you home," Randall said. "You know I worry about you, Ellie."

"I won't drink any more tonight. No lectures, I'm fine. By the way, what's with you being all chummy with Michael? You don't even know him, and now he's trying to buy our company for three quarters of what it's worth."

"It's the full net worth."

"It's worth more, especially when you consider the clients with outstanding contracts."

"I agree, but he's not the one deciding the numbers, Ellie. It's his uncle. He's just the messenger."

"So?"

"So if we get on his good side, then maybe he'll go to battle for us." Randall sipped his beer.

"Really? You believe that? You don't know much about business. There are no good sides. I've learned that the hard way, you know that."

"I guess we'll see then. I'll choose to remain positive.

"Tell me, does getting on Michael's good side involve using me as a bargaining chip?"

Randall leaned back, a wounded look on his face. "What the hell?"

She wrinkled her brow and studied his face.

"Seriously, Elle. Never in a million years would I do that to you and it pisses me off that you think that." His words were barely over a whisper.

"Well, why were you trying to persuade me to come along so hard today?"

"If you must know, he has a thing for you, and I think you have a thing for him. It's about time you should be dating again. As a matter of fact, it's about *damn* time. It's been two years since Ron died. Besides, in the end, who really cares if they buy us or not? It's not like it will be the end of the world if they don't. Sure, more money would be good, but we'll still get by."

Elle stared at Randall. "Who *are* you? Aren't you the one that wanted to hold out for more?"

"I've been reading this book Marcie gave me. It's about living in the present, living in the *now*."

"*The Power of Now*? I'm impressed. Yes, I'm quite familiar with it."

"It's good stuff."

"Agreed. She's a smart cookie. It's a good thing

you married her. So what makes you think Michael has a thing for me? More importantly, what makes you think I have a thing for him?" Elle absently twirled a piece of hair in her fingers.

"Because he asked my permission earlier to invite you to lunch tomorrow."

"He did? He actually asked your permission?" Elle couldn't decide whether Michael's gesture was chivalrous or just weird. "I guess that's nice, right?"

Randall smiled, and nodded. "It's old school."

"Well, he hasn't asked *my* permission yet."

"Jäger shots?" Tom inquired, as he approached with four shots, two in each hand. He sat down in the empty armchair.

"I'm out," Elle said, waving her hand.

"But I insist," Tom answered, placing one on the ottoman in front of her. "I remember how much you liked Jäger in high school."

Elle shot a look at her brother, who merely shrugged. "Well, you did."

"Okay, maybe this one," she conceded. "Cheers."

****

When Michael returned, he slid quietly into the empty spot next to Elle on the couch. "What's this?" he asked as a shot glass was placed in his hand. He sniffed it suspiciously.

"Jäger," grumbled Elle. "Tom insists."

"Ah, so it is." Michael hadn't tasted Jägermeister since college, and the smell reminded him of too many drunken parties. And toilet bowls.

Yeah, one toilet bowl too many, grimaced Michael as he swallowed the vile shot. Before he could fully recover, another was placed in front of him. Two were

43

enough, and he decided that once every ten years was often enough for drinking Jäger. He hoped his face hadn't betrayed the revulsion he'd felt too much, but then he'd never had a good poker face.

Conversation briefly visited religion before moving on to politics and most of the other taboo subjects Michael normally refused to discuss, especially with potential employees, so he paid attention instead. Actually, most of his attention was paid to Elle, who appeared to be getting a little tired. He liked how she giggled at every little thing. She was very cute, and even more so when she was relaxed. He couldn't remember ever seeing Sandra giggle. Sure, she'd laughed a few times, but it was a polite laugh, not a girly, honest laugh like Elle's.

Eventually Tom went home, leaving just the three of them. Randall asked the waitress to bring Elle some water.

"Ellie, you better let me drive you home," Randall said.

"I'm perfectly okay. I've only had two beers and two shots, perfectly spaced out over three hours, with food."

Randall glared at her.

"Fine," she relented, "but what about Monstro?"

"We'll come get it tomorrow."

"Monstro?" asked Michael.

The waitress returned with a glass of water for Elle, and Michael asked her for the bill.

Randall turned to Michael. "We're going to drop Ellie off at home first. It's on the way. Then I'll take you back to your hotel."

"I told him I'm fine," she insisted, turning to

Michael. "I hate leaving Monstro here overnight."

"Monstro?" asked Michael again.

"Her Jeep," answered Randall.

Michael thought for half a second. "I can drive Monstro. I'll drive you home."

"It's a stick," Elle warned.

"I do know how to drive a stick," Michael reassured her with a smile.

She narrowed her eyes at Michael and looked at her brother, who merely shrugged again.

The waitress arrived with the final bill, which Michael paid.

"It's settled then," he said, and winked at Elle.

Chapter Five

The first thing Michael had to do after squeezing behind the wheel was slide the seat all the way back.

"Oh, I forgot. I found this today and meant to give it to you," Elle said, handing him a piece of printed paper that had been lying on the passenger seat when she got in. He looked at it:

"Patience, Action, and Leadership. In Native American culture, the Puma spirit guide reminds us to patiently assess the situation and strike at the right opportunity. A wild mountain lion will concentrate on her prey, with stillness and patience, until she can anticipate its next move. If you are lucky enough to walk through a mountain lion's sacred space, consider yourself blessed with this message from the Great Spirit: "Take heed to meditate in stillness before pouncing, or what you desire may escape you."

"I don't know, I thought you'd find that interesting," she said, shrugging her shoulders.

He did in fact find it interesting, and even more interesting that she had thought to bring it to him. It was a kind gesture, and it had been a long time since a woman had done something thoughtful for him. Sandra was only nice to him when she wanted to borrow his credit card for some shopping trip. *Probably to buy underwear for Mark to see her in.* He shuddered involuntarily.

"You cold?" Elle asked.

"Um, no. Thank you for this. Truly." He carefully folded the paper and placed it in his shirt pocket, then twisted the key in the ignition. Elle pressed a button on the dash, and Michael jumped at the noise blasting from the speakers.

She giggled and turned it down to a more reasonable level. "Ah, sorry. Gotta love Living Dead!"

"A friend once told me, 'never apologize for rocking out.'"

"That's a wise friend."

"Buckle up, wild child." He grinned at her.

A few miles down the road, she turned to him. "This is actually pretty embarrassing because I feel perfectly fine. Randall worries too much."

"That's what older brothers are supposed to do."

"I guess so. Do you have siblings?"

"Me? No, I'm an only child. But you know, if I did, I'd have my little sister's back all the time."

"Ugh, you have no idea how unreasonable he can be, and how annoying!"

"I have some idea. We have something in common, we're both men."

"Yeah, I guess you do," she murmured. "So…your place or mine?"

He flashed back to the dream he'd had that morning, and eyed her quickly.

"I mean, well, obviously I'm not driving tonight so we'll end up in one place or the other…"

"I was planning to call a cab from your place," he said.

"You know, getting a cab in Denver isn't like hailing one in New York. It could take hours for one to show up. I learned that once when I had to go to the airport and almost missed my flight. It was a nightmare. You could stay at my place tonight, if you want, since it's so late already. I have coffee and bagels." She saw his look. "Yep, good New York-style bagels, with lox and cream cheese, even. But you're on the couch, of course."

"All right, you twisted my arm with the bagels." He casually pulled his cell phone out of his pocket and checked it. No missed calls. "You've had New York bagels... Have you been there?"

"Of course, hasn't everyone?"

"You'd be surprised. So you like New York?"

"Well, I don't see how anyone could live there long term. It's so...big and anonymous, but maybe there is something to that. It'd be nice to be anonymous sometimes, that's for sure. And it'd be nice to be able to visit the museums whenever you want."

"There are some advantages to anonymity for sure, but we New Yorkers band together when we need to."

"I've noticed that. I saw what happened when that hurricane hit. Everyone was helping everyone. It really was a beautiful thing."

"What did you do when you visited?"

"I've done the tourist thing a few times. The Statue of Liberty, museums, shopping. I was there for New Year's Eve once, which was an absolutely crazy time. Oh, and the food! Oh my god, the food is amazing. Even the snack carts on every corner are delicious. Someday I'll go back and try more restaurants."

"Speaking of traveling, have you heard from Randall's partner? What did you say his name was?"

Elle smacked his arm lightly. "Nope, I'm not that

tipsy. You aren't getting anything out of me. These lips are sealed."

It's her. Definitely her.

"So where do you live? In Manhattan?" she asked.

"No, I live in Queens. I have an apartment in a brownstone. Third story. I was lucky and took over a rent-controlled lease. I got it for a steal."

"Nice. I've never been to Queens. I've been to Brooklyn, though, to the Art Museum."

"That's a great museum. Queens is about the same as Brooklyn, appearance-wise. Brooklyn seems to be the hip place to live lately though, which is another reason why I prefer Queens."

"You're not a trend follower?"

"Only market trends."

****

Elle's place was in a gated subdivision on the outskirts of town. She reached above his head and hit the remote on the sun visor, and the verdigris-colored gates slowly parted. A rabbit scampered across the road in front of them.

She had a single-story house a few blocks down on the right from the gate. The garage was neatly organized with plastic storage bins, and Michael noticed that there were two mountain bikes hung from the ceiling, one black and one purple.

"Well, here we are," she said as she pushed open the door to the laundry room and turned the alarm off. She flipped on the light switch and led him inside. Michael inspected the abstract canvas paintings hanging in the hall and the living room. The signature was a series of loops and curls, and he didn't recognize it.

"Who is the artist?" he asked, admiring a green

one.

"Do you like them?"

"These two I do, and the orange one in the hallway, but I didn't really care for the blue one," he said honestly.

"They're mine," she said, smiling proudly.

"Did I mention I love the blue one?"

She laughed. "It's okay. I painted it at a bad time in my life. You must have picked up on that." She plopped down on the overstuffed white loveseat with one foot curled under her. He eased himself onto the matching sofa and tried to appear relaxed, even though all of his senses were ultra-heightened. He felt like a fox in a chicken coop.

He glanced around the room, taking it all in. She had a large screen TV, and the walls were painted in shades of tan. There was a fireplace with a collection of multicolored glass vases on the mantel, above which rested a colorful abstract painting of hers. Two bookcases stood guard on either side, one filled with books, the other with DVDs. A housecat, seemingly in no hurry at all, ambled into the living room and curled up in front of the fireplace.

"That's George," said Elle. "So can I get you something? Water? Soda? Tea?"

"Sure, water. Thanks."

She kicked her boots off and padded to the kitchen, returning with a glass of water and setting it on the pine coffee table in front of him.

"Ah, damn it," she gasped, suddenly sinking down on the couch next to him and clutching her left foot. "Foot cramp." She inhaled through clenched teeth. "I haven't had one of these in a long time." She groaned and rubbed her foot.

"Are you okay?"

"I think I've got it," she said, slowly moving her hand away from her foot. She tried to stand, only to fall sideways back onto the sofa. "I guess not. How embarrassing."

"Not at all. Here, let me try." He placed a throw pillow on his lap. She cautiously stretched her leg out and offered her foot, tensing her muscles and grimacing. He found the tender knot on the sole of her foot. He gently pressed it, and she winced.

"Holy crap!" cried Elle. She punched the couch, but didn't pull her foot away.

"Just give it a minute. Try to relax," he said in a low voice. She inhaled through her teeth again and covered her face with her hands. He kept steady pressure on the knot, slowly moving his finger in circles until she relaxed and removed her hands from her face.

Elle rubbed her foot and grinned slightly. "Ah, that feels much better already," she said with a sigh. She really was amazed that he was able to work the kink out so easily, and so quickly. She couldn't help but wonder how talented his hands might be in other places as well. "It's a good thing you were here. Otherwise, I might have just curled up in the fetal position all by myself. Thank you."

"You're welcome," he said.

Elle leaned forward, picked up the remote from the coffee table, turned on the TV and scanned for something interesting. She settled on a sci-fi B movie about abominable snowmen, then shrugged and set the remote gently back in its place.

"How often to do you have a cramp like that?" he

asked.

"Oh, every once in a while," she answered. "I'm always afraid I'll get one at a really bad time, like when I'm driving."

"Or when you're trying to outrun a bear?"

She laughed and reached over to knock on the table. "Don't jinx me!"

On the TV, an abominable snowman attacked and killed some unfortunate actor. The poor man's head, torn from his body, rolled across the snow like a bloody bowling ball.

"Would you like me to rub the other one, too, just in case?"

"Free foot rubs? Sure."

He took hold of her other foot.

"Michael, do you get manicures?"

He stopped rubbing for a second. "I have a few times. Why?"

"I thought so; your hands are really smooth for a man."

"Is this too hard?" He applied more pressure.

She tensed up for a second, then relaxed again. "No, it's fine."

He turned back to the TV, his jaw clenched and bent her left leg up slightly and placed his hands behind her knee. "I should get your calves, too, that's where the tension comes from."

He glided his hands expertly up and down her left calf, using gentle pressure on the muscles then stopped abruptly, sat back against the pillows and started to tell her about the muscles and ligaments of the leg, and how they were all connected to the foot in an intricate pattern.

She was glad he did, she needed to move her brain away from its current train of thought. She'd wanted to swing her legs over his shoulder and watch him bury his head between them.

"Where did you learn all that?" she asked.

"In college."

"You're a doctor?" She almost laughed. "Are you an astronaut, too?"

"No. Not quite. I actually wanted to be a chiropractor, and went to school for a couple years. Then I fell into the job at my uncle's agency, and everything took off from there. And here I am."

"Yes, here you are, rubbing my calves and telling me all about the muscles and ligaments in my legs. Are you happy at your job?"

"Happy? I suppose I am. It pays well, and I have a pretty good life in New York, all things considered."

"But…"

"But well…like you said, here I am telling you I wanted to be a chiropractor."

She sat up. "I think it's time I go to bed."

He stood up with her.

"Do you want to go to lunch tomorrow?" he asked abruptly.

"Yes! I mean, sure. That sounds good."

"Good."

"Okay. The bathroom is down the hall, the icemaker rattles sometimes, and George might want to get a bit friendly. I'll go grab you a pillow and blanket," she said, then suddenly leaned in and gave him a quick, tight hug.

He almost lost his footing, and before he was able to return the embrace she slipped away, disappearing down the hall.

She came back and deposited a pillow and blanket on the couch.

"Good night again," she said, but didn't hug him a second time.

Michael finally composed himself and made his way down the hall to Elle's spare bathroom and splashed cold water on his face. After blotting it off with the hand towel, he stared in the mirror and tried to convince himself it would be a very bad idea to barge into her bedroom, pull her covers off and ravage her senseless. He smiled slightly at his reflection and shook his head. He hadn't felt like that since college. Nope, knocking down her door would be rather...*abrupt* would be a good word. He needed to focus his attention elsewhere if he were to get through the night. Or leave. Perhaps he should leave. But...

It was something he normally wouldn't do, but he felt compelled. He couldn't resist the temptation and gingerly opened the medicine cabinet, feeling like a complete asshole. Pain relievers, cold medicine, antacids, bandages, blister ointment, and condoms.

Condoms? He took out the box and examined it. Unopened and expired for a year. Ribbed for her pleasure, even. He put the box back in the cabinet and wiped his hand on his pant leg as he continued his survey.

A man's shaving and grooming set, aftershave, and a few half-empty bottles of cologne; one was the brand he used. There was also an electronic toothbrush and a partially used tube of toothpaste.

Of course, she had a boyfriend. She was beautiful and intelligent, how could she not? What if her boyfriend came over tonight and saw another man sleeping in her living room? As a matter of fact, why hadn't she called him to come pick her up from the Lodge? And why were her boyfriend's things in her spare bathroom instead of the master?

Perhaps she had a roommate? Sheesh, there were some things the Internet was good for and some things it wasn't. Randall hadn't said she was taken when he'd asked. Yet he decided he'd still go with the lunch date plan. She'd already said yes. He also decided it was late, and he had better come to his senses and call a cab after all. After calling, he sat on her sofa in the dark for a bit, watching the clock, waiting for the twenty minutes to go by that the cab company had told him it would take. He decided he'd better leave her a note, so he went to the kitchen and switched on the light to find a piece of paper and a pen.

On the fridge he noticed a grouping of pictures. Elle at the Grand Canyon with a good-looking man in dreadlocks. Elle and Randall in their younger days. A receipt from a pest control company. Elle in a bathing suit on a tropical beach somewhere with a coconut drink in her hand. She appeared quite comfortable and cozy, and she looked great in the red bikini. He leaned in to examine the picture closer.

Again, he was glad he'd called the cab.

****

Elle slid down, her back against her bedroom door as soon as it clicked closed. She hoped Michael wouldn't peek in the medicine cabinet in the spare bathroom; she didn't want to have to explain anything. She didn't care if he looked anywhere else in her house; she had nothing to hide, except for what was in there.

She didn't want to have that conversation with him. Not yet.

After putting her pajamas on, she went to her en suite, brushed her teeth and washed her face. The warm washcloth felt really good against her skin. A sample of soy-based night cream had come in the mail earlier, so she decided to try it.

After turning off the light and sinking into bed, a sliver of light shone through the bottom of the door and she realized he had turned the kitchen light on. She should go out there, but why?

Water. That's a good reason.

She stood and opened her door.

"Hey, you lost?" she asked as she walked toward the kitchen.

He looked startled; he had been studying the pictures on the fridge. She noticed it was the one of her trip to Cabo in the red bikini.

"I decided to call a cab after all."

"Did you? Okay then, no bagel for you." She hoped her tone didn't convey the disappointment she felt.

Disappointment? It wasn't like he had been in her bed, and she didn't want him to be either, did she? She opened a cabinet, retrieved a glass and set it under the water dispenser on the fridge, waiting for it to fill.

Headlights shone through the living room windows as a cab pulled in her driveway.

"Wow, that was fast," she remarked.

"I'll give you a call in the morning, okay?"

"Sure." She figured the less communication, the better and didn't look up as he walked out her door.

George rubbed against her leg after she locked the

door. "Sorry, bud, it's just you and me again. Nothing new there." She reached down to scratch his ears, and then picked him up and headed off to bed.

Chapter Six

Elle was surprised to feel such acute disappointment that Michael wasn't lying on the couch in the morning, but grinned, remembering how awkward he had seemed. Perhaps she still had that effect on guys. She also remembered the impromptu foot massage, and the way his hands felt on her skin. A tingle shot to her core, and she straightened and tried to ignore it.

She was bent over, drying her hair, when her phone rang and her whole body jolted. Her phone hardly ever rang lately, and the volume was too danged loud. The noise still caught her off guard every time a call came through because she remembered the many calls from the hospital when Ron was sick. Each time the hospital number had displayed on the caller ID, she'd steeled her nerves thinking it was "the call."

She switched off her blow dryer and answered.

"Hey, Elle, it's Michael."

"Oh, hey. Um, good morning." She fussed with her hair in the mirror.

"Are you feeling okay?"

"Yep, yep, all good. Thank you again for driving me home last night. It really wasn't necessary."

"That's all right. You were fine. So, about lunch…"

"Yeah?" She twirled the phone cord in her fingers.

"I hear there's a nice café near the Denver Art Museum. It seems we both like art. How does that sound?"

"I know the place well. That sounds great."

"Okay, so I'll pick you up at, say...noon?"

"All right."

"See ya then."

After finishing drying her hair, she plugged her curling iron in to let it heat up while she contemplated the closet. She felt no real concern over the sensibility of agreeing to this lunch date, but she did fret for a while over what she was going to wear.

She decided on her lucky jeans, black wedge heels and a fuchsia-colored top with lace edges.

"How's this look?" she asked George when she'd dressed and curled her hair. She twisted her hair in her fingers and stared at the housecat, who gazed lazily back at her from her pillow. "That good, huh? Well, it'll have to do."

Perfume? No, she decided not to. This wasn't really a date anyways. Or was it? She resolved to pay for her part of the meal. After all, if he paid for her, then it was a date, and if they each paid for themselves then it wasn't. It was silly logic, but she decided to go with it.

At exactly noon, the doorbell rang.

Prompt. Of course, George couldn't be bothered to move from her pillow to see her off.

As they drove, Michael's cell phone rang, but he ignored it. A minute later, it rang again.

"Your phone...aren't you going to answer it?"

He glanced at the screen. "It's New York. I'm busy, and they can wait."

Elle felt a grin curl her lips, knowing he ignored business for her company. "You're not originally from New York, are you?"

"No, but I've lived there eight years already. It feels like home. Where do you think I'm from?" He glanced in her direction and smiled. She hadn't noticed he had a dimple before.

She shook her head. "I have no idea. I can't detect an accent."

"We'll let it remain a mystery then."

"Yeah, I…" Elle started, then suddenly sat upright. "What cologne is that?"

"It's Pasha. Why?"

It had sent a shock through her body, and she groaned quietly.

****

"Are you allergic or something? I'm sorry, I didn't know. I didn't use much." *Ah, crap, it was one of the bottles I saw in her spare bathroom.*

She shook her head and wrinkled her brow. "No, no it's not that. Don't worry, it smells great. It's just…well, that's what my husband wore."

Michael paused to brace himself. "I didn't know you were married," he said, surprised and dismayed that his internet research hadn't drudged up evidence of a marriage.

"I'm not. I mean, I was, but I'm not anymore." She took a deep breath. "I'm sorry. I just haven't smelled that cologne for a while."

Elle's body language changed, and she leaned toward the window for the rest of the ride. She seemed entirely preoccupied, and Michael felt a bit awkward. When they entered the restaurant, she was polite and courteous, and when he suggested they sit on the patio, she'd agreed with a smile. He decided to keep playing it cool and perhaps the date would improve as time wore on.

She ordered a seafood salad with a lemon San Pellegrino to drink. He ordered the lobster ravioli, remembering it from a previous trip. When the food arrived, the dish was as delicious as he'd recalled, yet he couldn't fully enjoy it without clearing the air first.

"Why don't you ask me the big burning question?" Elle's voice sliced into his thoughts.

"Huh?" Michael blinked, looking up.

"You know... 'Since you're not married anymore, when did you get divorced?'"

Michael shifted uncomfortably. "I...uh..."

"It's okay. I'd rather get it out than deal with the giant pink elephant anymore. You see, I'm a widow."

"But you're so young." Michael felt like an asshole as soon as he said the words. *I didn't see that one coming. How could I have missed it, and why didn't Randall give me a head's up?*

She took a deep breath. "Ron passed away about two years ago. He had cancer."

Michael pushed his plate away and folded his hands. "I'm so sorry, Elle. You don't have to tell me any more if you don't want to." *Damn Internet isn't good for anything but losing time going down rabbit holes.*

"It's all right. I don't mind talking about it."

Michael groped for something to say. "Was that his mountain bike in your garage?" He finally asked. He'd never known a young widow and wasn't sure how to proceed.

61

Elle smiled. "Yes, I couldn't bring myself to get rid of it yet. The Jeep was his, too. I also kept some of his bathroom stuff, but I moved it to the spare bathroom. It's funny, the things you find you're attached to and the things you aren't." She paused to steady her voice.

"I painted a lot when he was sick. The blue one in the hallway, I painted that when he was near the end. It helped put things in perspective, to organize my thoughts. It was kind of like a journal, but without words, because there were no words. It felt really good to come home from the hospital and paint."

"I bet it did. He was a very lucky man to have you, Elle," Michael said.

"Thank you."

"So as long as I'm being inappropriate...have you always known you're adopted?"

"Yes, I have, and I don't mind you asking that either. You'll have to try harder than that to offend me. I'm an artist, remember?"

"Have you ever looked for your parents?"

"I know exactly where they are. They're in Greenwood Cemetery in San Diego."

"And there I go again," he said. But he would be sure to remember her hometown.

She continued, "I was three. Jake and my father had been friends since they were kids. Jake and Patty were living in San Diego at the time. They were babysitting me the night of the accident. My parents had gone to a fundraiser in Laguna, and their car ran into oncoming traffic on the way back. Someone said there was a stray dog in the street and they swerved to avoid hitting it. The delivery truck coming from the opposite direction didn't swerve, and hit their car straight on. They were both dead by the time the ambulance arrived."

"That must have been so horrible for you," Michael said.

"It was. I mean, I can remember bits and pieces. I was really young, but I remember being in foster care for a while. You know, bureaucracy." She rolled her eyes and pointed east over her shoulder toward Washington, DC. "Jake and Patty visited me all the time, petitioned to adopt me, and were finally granted it since I had no other living relatives. Then Jake moved us out here to Denver so we could have a fresh start together as a family."

"What do you remember about your parents?" He leaned in, genuinely interested.

"Not much. But my father was a businessman, like you," she said. "And my mother, she stayed at home with me. She was an artist. I remember she would finger paint with me, using all of the colors at once." Elle's gaze drifted off. "I guess that's why I started painting. I wanted to keep her memory alive."

"She would be very proud of you, I'm sure of it."

"Thank you. Tell me, how is it that you are single? I'm assuming you are, of course."

"Well, apparently I have this huge biohazard symbol tattooed on my forehead. It keeps women away." He pulled his hair back with his other hand to expose a bare forehead.

Elle laughed, exposing a dimple.

Good. Progress.

"Excuse me," intruded the waiter, "but my shift is about to end and I wanted to leave this. No rush, please enjoy yourselves." He placed the bill on the table between them, a bit closer to Michael than Elle. She reached for it, but Michael caught her hand beneath his.

"I insist," he said.

"And what if I also insist?"

Michael pondered a moment. "Do you know rock, paper, scissors?"

"Are you serious?"

"I'm always serious," he said soberly, his hand still covering hers.

"Hmm, perhaps you need to get out more. All right, you count." She withdrew her hand from the bill. They played the game, and his rock crushed her scissors.

"I'd like to test that theory someday," she said.

"What?" He studied the bill, and reached for a pen.

"Try to crush a pair of scissors with a rock. That would take a really long time. I don't think it's a very accurate game."

"It depends on the size of the rock."

"So you're saying size matters?" she asked playfully.

"Oh, most definitely," he replied, never looking up from the bill.

Chapter Seven

Elle believed that everything happened for a reason, and it was not a fluke that Michael wore the same cologne that Ron had. His closeness that afternoon as they strolled through the museum made her feel comforted and peaceful, as if it were a sign Ron was finally releasing her from mourning. She imagined that Ron would have liked him, even though he didn't appear to have an outdoorsy bone in his body. He was genuine and seemed honest, and those were qualities that Ron would appreciate in a friend.

The halls were familiar, like an old friend she hadn't visited with for a long time. She used to make frequent trips to the museum when Ron was alive and they'd been members, but she hadn't renewed her membership since he'd passed away. Strolling into one room in particular surprised her as she realized they'd altered the collection on view. Regular trips to the museum should become part of her usual agenda again, she resolved, as well as making a mental note to renew her membership. It felt good to be there again.

"I know it's not as wonderful or breathtaking as the Met," she said as they walked into another viewing room.

"Well, you can't judge art by its surroundings, but the Met does have a much larger collection, of course. You can have a Monet in a warehouse or a mansion, and it's still a Monet."

"I've never thought of it that way." They stood silently, both lost in their own thoughts.

Presently, Michael asked, "So you've been to New York?"

"You asked that exact question last night, silly. Of course I've been to New York."

"Yeah, I guess I did, and I seem to recall you weren't impressed."

"Oh, not at all; I absolutely loved it. It's so inspiring and energetic." She looked into his eyes. "But I can't imagine living there. It must be grueling."

Yeah, I heard you say that last night. Michael loved New York, but he had to admit to a certain fondness for his hometown, especially recently. They stopped in front of Monet's *Waterloo Bridge*.

"You enjoy art, then?" Elle questioned.

"Yes, I do. Sometimes when I have a free Sunday afternoon, I stroll through the Met or the MoMA. I'm a bit spoiled to have so many amazing museums to choose from. Have you ever visited the Morgan?"

"I've never heard of that one."

"You're kidding! It's one of the best. It's small, but it houses the most amazing original manuscripts and handwritten sheet music. It is Pierpont Morgan's private library and art collection. It's amazing. You're familiar with JP Morgan?"

"Of course."

"That's his son. He realized what treasures his dad had collected and turned it into an amazing showcase."

"You seem to have a certain fondness for it." Elle smiled, melting him.

"I do. It's a beautiful thing to me, the fact that he

collected these priceless treasures in order to keep them safe. And his dream was for the public to be able to admire and study them. And now, so many years after his death, his dream is still alive."

"That's beautiful. Okay, I'm convinced. I'm finding the Morgan Museum on my next visit for sure."

"You should. You won't be disappointed." He felt like squeezing her, but didn't.

"It's much easier than you think," she whispered, leaning close to him.

He stared at the Monet in front of him. "What's much easier than I think?"

"Painting. You should try it some time."

"I'm no good at art. I can't even draw a straight line, but I appreciate those that can."

"Nonsense. Draw what you see. Trust what your eyes tell you is there and copy it."

He turned to her. "I do trust what my eyes tell me. I just don't trust my hands."

"There's nothing wrong with your hands, they worked pretty well on my feet last night." Her cheeks flushed. "You should come over and paint with me sometime. I'm curious to see what you would come up with."

"Ever see a pissed-off monkey? That's me, with paint. I can't even paint a wall without getting half of it on the ceiling and the other half on my shirt sleeves."

She guffawed, making some people turn their heads. She took his hand. "Come on, let's go outside."

If she kept holding his hand, he decided he would follow her anywhere, maybe even to the ends of the Earth. She squeezed with gentle, solid pressure until they were out the front door. They found a bench under a tree to sit on.

"Let me see something." She turned his palm up and began tracing her index finger up and down the lines in the middle of it.

"You're a palm reader, too?"

"Not really, but I do know a little about it. See this line here? That's your lifeline. No, it doesn't mean how long you will live. It means your life's purpose. Basically, whether or not you are focused or scattered. You are focused, but you already knew that. See how solid it is? And this one, this is your money line. I think we both know what that one says."

"What does it say?"

"It says you're dirt poor and miserable, you always will be, and there isn't a charitable, kind bone in your body. You're an insufferable jerk, for sure." She met his eyes and grinned. "Only kidding."

"Sounds true enough." He shrugged.

She looked down again. "Ah, but this next one is very interesting."

"Come on, don't tease me. Tell me the bad news," he said, even though he enjoyed her teasing and the soft touch of her finger on his palm. He started to imagine her hand elsewhere, and then quickly shut off that line of thinking as he didn't want to embarrass himself when they eventually stood up.

"Fine. This is your love line. It's scattered and broken many times."

"Well, that's no good, is it?"

"It's not all bad..." She paused dramatically. "See here? All the little loops and curves come together and form one solid deep line until the end. It means after years of searching you will finally find someone that you will love deeply for the rest of your life."

Michael felt lightheaded and saw spots in front of his eyes again, like he had the first day he met her on the trail when they saw the mountain lion. Elle continued to trace her finger along his love line, from end to end.

He took her hand and turned it over, examining her palm and comparing it to his own.

"That one," Elle answered and pointed, as if she had read his mind. Her love line started as a short series of loops, and then broke into a solid line that tapered off in a downward arc. Another deep, solid line started where that one broke and continued to wrap around the side of her hand like his did. Michael didn't need formal palm reader training to come up with a good idea of what it meant.

"Can I buy you dinner tonight?" Michael wrapped both his hands over hers.

"Dinner? You just bought me lunch."

"I know, but I like to plan ahead, and so far I don't want this day to end."

Elle flushed. "Unfortunately, I already have plans for tonight. I'm supposed to meet Elizabeth at six." She turned her hand over to glance at her watch. "Oh, wow, that's in an hour, I've lost track of time. We'd better get back."

"Elizabeth?" he asked as they walked toward his rental car.

"Ah…you don't know her." An uneasy silence followed.

"Right," he finally said. *Maybe Elizabeth is the silent partner, and I've been completely wrong.* "Coffee tomorrow morning, then? My flight leaves at ten."

"I have class tomorrow morning."

"My loss," he said with a grin. "I'll be back on Thursday afternoon. Perhaps then?"

"Maybe," she laughed and tilted her head back a little, the sun glinting off the tips of her blonde hair as she slid into the passenger seat.

****

As Michael walked her to her front door, Elle noticed that she felt quite nervous. Was he planning to kiss her? It had been a long time since she'd been kissed, and what would she do if he did? Pass out? Hiccup? Laugh? Was her breath okay? Did she even remember how to kiss someone?

Was it appropriate to kiss him? Well, all things considered, if he kissed her, he was the one being inappropriate. He was the one fraternizing with the client's sister. She reminded herself that he didn't know he was fraternizing with the client.

If he kissed her, "inappropriate" would feel good.

Then again, she remembered that he'd obtained Randall's permission to bring her on the date today.

At her door she turned to him, her face square with his chest, and before she knew it he had pulled her to him, his chin resting on top of her head. She wrapped her arms around his waist. He smelled like Ron, and it was familiar and comforting, yet she was acutely aware that he wasn't Ron. No, the man holding her was Michael, someone she had only personally known for little more than a week, yet she felt like she had always known him, somehow. His hands moved to cradle the back of her head as he kissed her hair, then her forehead. She tilted her face up to his and their lips met in an unsteady, awkward kiss.

Elle's heart banged against her ribcage as relentlessly as a high school marching band in a competition. And then, it happened. She couldn't help it. It rose up from her stomach, carried by the butterflies, and before she knew it, it had escaped her mouth.

She giggled, loud and long.

"I'm sorry," she said, after composing herself. "I'm sorry, I really don't know where that came from." She cleared her throat and bit her lip.

"Well, I haven't had a girl laugh at me when I kissed her since elementary school. Let's try this again." He leaned in, and then just before their lips touched he leaned back again. "No laughing this time, Elle, this is very serious business."

Although she felt the beginnings of another nervous giggle, this one only rose as far as the back of her tongue. He had lifted her up slightly and somehow backed her up against the closed door. She was completely dazed by the time his mouth left hers and tried to catch her breath.

"Cancel your plans," he whispered in her ear and then kissed her below it. She felt his intention pressing hard against her thigh, and it was thoroughly tempting. It had been two years since she'd had sex, at least.

"I can't." *But God, I want to.*

"Denied. But it was worth a try," he murmured into her neck with a slight chuckle.

"Elizabeth is only going to be here a few days. She's my best friend and Randall's sister-in-law. And she's probably already at the restaurant chomping at the bit to tell me all about life in Tucson," she said reluctantly, and breathlessly.

"Understood. I learned a long time ago never to get between a woman and her friends." He stepped back so that she could unlock her door.

"You have my number, right?" he asked.

"Yes."

"Call me. Or text."

"I will."

"Drive safe."

She thought about asking Michael to come to dinner, too, but knew that she wouldn't be able to give her friend her full attention if he was there.

Besides, in light of recent events, she really needed her bestie.

****

"'It's nice?' I need something better than that to go on," Elizabeth said quite loudly, making Elle temporarily forget her more pressing dilemma and focus on the heads that quickly turned in their direction.

"It's rounded, and he has a slight swagger when he walks. But not like an arrogant swagger, it's more like a casual swagger. Yeah, a casual walk. Is that detailed enough?" Elle responded in a whisper as the onlookers went back to their own business.

"Casual, or relaxed-and-in-charge swagger?" She leaned in, hand on her chin.

"In charge. Definitely in charge."

"You know how those in-charge men are in the bedroom? You ready for that *Fifty Shades* action?"

She blushed.

Elizabeth touched her cheek. "Well, I think that's a yes." She leaned back, got the waiter's attention and ordered a second drink.

"'Rounded?' That's somewhat descriptive, you're

getting better," she said with a smile. "Okay, now tell me the real stuff. When are you going to tell him who you are?"

"I'm scared to, Elizabeth. I really like him. What if it screws everything up if he knows I've been lying this whole time?"

"He's going to find out eventually. It's better now than later, right? You should have never let Randall talk you into it. It hasn't been that long yet, only a few weeks. Besides, you aren't exactly lying. He just hasn't asked the right questions."

"Yes, he has. When we went on the hike, the first day I met him, he asked me straight up if I was the partner."

"He did? And what did you say?"

"I said they were out of the country. He assumes it's a man."

"Sexist."

"No, that's not like him. If I were in his shoes, I'd probably assume the same thing."

"Hmm, if you say so. And you did lie to him. When are you going to tell him the truth?"

"I wanted to tell him today, but I couldn't. I was happy just being with him, and I didn't want to ruin it." She sighed. "I haven't felt like this about anyone since Ron."

"You're a little ahead of yourself aren't you?"

"I know it. It's stupid, huh?"

"No, it's not stupid. You need some happiness in your life. It's about damn time. Talk to him, honey, but take it slow."

"I will," she said. "Tomorrow."

Elizabeth leaned over and squeezed her hand

gently. "While you're at it, find out if he has a brother with a nice rear end."

"Sorry to disappoint you, but he's an only child."

"Figures. My luck." She shrugged.

"What about you, Elizabeth? Any new men in your life?"

"Well"—she took a breath and let it out slowly—"let me tell you about the last nightmare date I was on."

"Oh no, what happened this time?"

"First he made me drive all the way to his side of town, which was the complete opposite side of town for me. Then, he didn't even offer to pay for my drink. Can you believe that?"

"Geez."

"I know. I should have left. But morbid curiosity kept me there. I wanted to see what else he'd do."

"And…?"

Elizabeth grabbed Elle's arm. "Ha! He proceeded to describe to me in detail the many things he hated about his ex-wife and regretted about their relationship."

"Groovy."

"Yeah. I handed him my shrink's card, then left."

Chapter Eight

Asshole, asshole, asshole, Michael chanted to himself as he grabbed a beer out of his fridge. He'd just gotten home from his usual Monday flight and collapsed into the love seat, taking a long swig of the brew.

What the hell am I doing, trying to sleep with the client? Assuming she is, in fact, the client. Maybe it's Elizabeth. Either way, Elle is the sister of the client, that is beyond doubt, and that is bad enough.

Michael was walking a tightrope and he couldn't help it. He felt dangerous and a bit like a stranger in his own skin, but it felt good for a change. The thought of going into his uncle's office the next morning seemed like it belonged in someone else's story, not his, and Elle had picked up on that. He thought he'd hidden his dissatisfaction better than that, yet she *saw* him. That made him afraid and curious at the same time.

Still, maybe her questioning his happiness was merely conversational. Maybe he was looking too far into it. It was plausible that he wanted her to *see* him so badly he was willing to believe her casual question was something deeper. Jesus, he was starting to think like…

Like a girl.

But he couldn't stop it. Besides, there was no reason why he shouldn't be allowed to think and feel. With Sandra, he hadn't been allowed. If he'd ever

75

shown a sliver of emotion she'd laugh it off. What kind of woman did that? A woman that would sleep with their realtor, that's whom. He had played the role of dutiful significant other until it became second nature, but with Elle it was different. Every little thing she said set him off in some way, whether it was a spark of anger, a twinge of memory, or some train of thought that led him down an unfamiliar and exciting path. She was full of surprises, and she had his full attention. He had never been so affected by a woman, and he'd only known her for a short time. He wondered if her magnetism would ever wear off.

She had magic.

****

Early Monday morning, Elle called Randall to tell him she needed to talk. He invited her to lunch, but she reminded him she had class so they decided she would come over that evening for dinner. That way she could have some more time with Elizabeth while she was there. It seemed she'd hardly seen her that visit.

Elle stopped at the store to pick up a six-pack of microbrew. When she arrived at Randall's house, the Scrabble board on the coffee table told her a game was nearing completion. Randall played his last three tiles and Elizabeth went to the kitchen to help her sister with dinner.

"I don't think you won that game fair. Twat isn't a word, my dear brother," Elle said sweetly.

"It's in the dictionary. Trust me. Besides, Lizzy didn't argue." Randall smiled.

"That's only because she's hungry."

"Likely." Randall cleared the Scrabble board and leaned back on the couch.

"Did you buy a new cell phone yet?" Elle asked, as she handed him a bottle.

"Yes, I finally gave in," he answered.

"That's good."

Marcie came in to say hello and took the rest of the pack to the kitchen.

Randall took a swig of beer. "Now, what is it you wanted to talk to me about, sis?"

"Well, I've been doing some thinking, and I really think we should accept their new offer. It's pretty fair, even considering the outstanding contracts we have."

"I completely agree."

Elle's jaw gaped. "You do?"

"Uh-huh. I mean, it's more than I thought they would offer, and he seems like a decent guy. We have yet to meet John Steele, but I've spoken to him on the phone numerous times, as you know. Also, they're adding the agreement to maintain the current staff."

Elle slid off the couch to the floor and crossed her arms over her knees, which were drawn up to her chest. "Well, I guess it's time to make the call then."

Randall tapped his foot and stared into the distance for a moment. "You know, even though I know it's the right thing, it feels weird. It's like we're giving up."

"No, Randall, it's not like that. I think we should look at it as revitalization."

"Maybe."

"Do you have doubts?"

Randall didn't respond.

She let her head sink between her hands. "Ugh, me, too," she groaned. "Holding the livelihoods of so many people we care about is a big responsibility. Once we sign on that line, it's over."

"Sis, I know it is the best thing, and you do, too. Dad has already told us his wishes. The only thing left to do is sign everything. We've got this. I'll call Michael first thing in the morning. I'd call him now, but it's probably too late already. It's already nine in New York." Randall was using his authoritative tone. He didn't use it very often, but when he did it meant that the argument was over, and he'd won. Elle rather liked this aspect of her brother's personality. He really was a great manager, when he was in the mood.

"Okay," she said. What else was there to say?

"So you didn't tell me, how the drive home went the other night...?"

"It was fine. He called a cab from my place." Elle decided to leave out the part about the foot rub.

"That's good. Very gentlemanly of him. Did he ever ask you to lunch?"

"Yeah he did, finally."

"Oh? And how did that go?" Randall asked.

"Yes, tell him how your lunch date was, Ellie." Elizabeth breezed into the room and sat on the love seat, one leg curled beneath her.

Elle blushed.

"That good, huh?" Randall teased.

"Shut up. Geez, you guys..." Elle laughed.

"Yeah, leave her alone, Liz." Randall elbowed his sister-in-law. "She's finally into someone. Finally."

"I know. She's just so...so cute." She reached over and gave her bestie a squeeze.

"I don't know, he was such a goof at first," said Elle. "That first day on the hike...total goof. But now, I don't know, something more?"

"I hear he's a good kisser..." Elizabeth trailed off.

"Gosh, look at her. She's like a preteen!" Randall teased his sister with a smile.

"…And I also hear that he has a nice ass," Elizabeth continued.

Elle cleared her throat and glanced around. "Okay, you guys. Enough. No more teasing me. In all seriousness…where's my beer?"

****

Back at home, Michael didn't sleep a wink on Monday night, but greeted Tuesday morning bright and early, intent on making a difference that day. Freshly showered, he wrapped a towel around his waist, picked his clothes up from the floor and put them in a bag to take to the dry cleaners.

He dressed in sweatpants and a T-shirt, then sat down in his office chair and called his secretary to check his schedule. Nothing was pressing until late afternoon, which meant he had the rest of the morning to himself, so he opened his planner app and began tapping out a list of things he needed to accomplish. In the first slot, he wrote, "Become a man worthy of Elle." He grabbed his dry cleaning, and on impulse, he reached to pull something else from the bottom of his closet. Michael blew the dust bunnies from his gym bag.

Al's Dry Cleaners was just around the corner from Michael's apartment. Michael had never met Al, but had always assumed the nice lady in her fifties that seemed to live behind the counter was Al's wife. As usual, she wrote out a ticket for him when he dropped off his laundry and found his clean clothes from the week before. But today, as he was headed out the door, he heard her call out to him.

"Yes?" he asked, walking back to the counter.

"You might want these," she said in a deep, manly voice while looking at him over the rim of her glasses. On the counter she laid out a pack of cigarettes and a folded piece of paper.

"Ah. Thanks." He took the items and headed back out the door. He realized he hadn't smoked a cigarette since Sunday morning, and he didn't particularly want one now. He tossed the half-full pack into the nearest garbage can and found a bench to sit down on so he could read the paper again.

Elle had printed it for him, with the symbolic meaning of the mountain lion. He unfolded the paper and read it thoroughly, lingering on the last sentence and read it over several times.

If you are lucky enough to walk through a mountain lion's sacred space, consider yourself blessed with this message from the Great Spirit: "Take heed to meditate in stillness before pouncing, or what you desire may escape you."

He refolded the paper and carefully tucked it inside his gym bag.

Well, first things first...

Michael entered the gym through the revolving door and placed his membership card and ID onto the counter. The pretty young blonde behind the counter took his cards and looked up at him, smiling pleasantly. Her name badge identified her as Amy.

"I'm sorry, Mr. Williams, but it appears your membership has expired."

"What?" He leaned over to look at the card. Amy showed him the expiration date was in March, five months ago.

"Would you like to renew now? We're having a special."

He ran his hand through his hair. "Sure." He was certain he'd been to the gym within the last five months, but now that he was thinking about it, maybe it had been longer. Damn, he'd been so busy that he hadn't even noticed spring had shifted to summer, and autumn was just around the corner.

Michael handed a credit card over and leaned against the counter, waiting for the transaction to process.

Amy smiled politely again and handed his card back to him. "I'm sorry, but this card has been declined."

Sandra. Goddamn it.

"Here, try this one," Michael said patiently, digging out a card he knew Sandra hadn't had access to. He mentally added a call to the bank to his list of tasks for the day.

She processed the second card easily. "Would you like the services of a trainer today, to show you the functions of our new machines?"

He shifted on his feet. The simple task of going to the gym was becoming a burden. Expired membership, new machines. What else?

"Yeah, why not?" He shrugged. His initial desire to exercise was quickly diminishing, but he tried to remain focused.

Michael's workout was mediocre at best, but at the end he consoled himself by calling it a good start. He mopped sweat from his eyes and checked his phone, and saw he'd missed a call from Randall's home residence. There was no message.

His heart sped back up as he showered, dressed, and went outside to find a quiet place to return the call. He ducked into a nearby bookshop and headed to the back. It was quiet, but it wasn't a library, so nobody was irritated over his short but intense conversation.

Randall and his partner were in. They wanted to meet John and close the deal as soon as possible. *Yes!* He was happy to have gotten that far with them, but also because it meant he would have a reason to see Elle again. If she was in fact the silent partner, he reminded himself. Oh hell, even if she wasn't, it didn't really matter much anymore and couldn't think of a better thing to happen that day, at least in regards to work.

Michael called his secretary to make reservations for Randall and Elle to be flown in and arranged for them to stay in a boutique hotel in SoHo as well as reserving Broadway tickets for the evening they arrived. They'd have a nice dinner somewhere, too, but he'd have to think about the location.

He hoped he could work in some alone time with Elle while she was there. Maybe he'd take her to the MoMA, or the Morgan Library. Yes, the Morgan Library, that would be the ideal place, and new to her. It would be right up her alley.

About an hour later he received the call from his secretary confirming the plane tickets were for Randall and Gabrielle. He thanked her and congratulated himself.

Gabrielle. It hadn't occurred to him that Elle could be short for Gabrielle. He liked it.

Later that evening when he finally arrived back home, tired but happy, Michael unfolded the printout from Elle and fastened it to the refrigerator with a magnet of the Denver skyline. He had purchased that magnet for Sandra long ago, but it was his now.

That night, Michael slept like a rock.

Chapter Nine

"What should I pack? I don't even know what to bring! Is it cold?" Elle rifled through her closet, examining each piece with a discerning eye before moving to the next.

Elizabeth lay back on the bed, watching her with amusement.

Elle turned. "I'm so glad you agreed to come with us."

"Me, too. It turned out the timing of this trip was just about perfect."

"You should let me buy your ticket though, really."

"No, no. I'm fine. It's all good. You just get yourself packed, lady." She stifled a chuckle, seeing her friend fuss over her clothes as much as she was. "We don't have all night. Five a.m. comes early, and I want at least a little bit of sleep first."

Elle sighed and pulled out a few pieces, set them on the bed, carefully folded them and placed them in her waiting carry-on. She retrieved her travel toiletries bag from under her sink, and some shoes from under her bed.

She rummaged around in her closet and held up a pair of black stilettos, with silver bands around the ankles. "These, too, do you think?"

Elizabeth leaned over and peeked in her carry-on. "Yeah, there's room. What are you going to wear them with?"

"If I wear them, I'll wear them with…this." She turned on her heels and showed her friend a little black dress with sequin trim at the bottom.

"Good choice. I approve." Elizabeth continued to observe her friend pack and it was almost as fascinating as a documentary film on silk worms. "By the way, how are things in San Diego lately?" she asked.

Elle paused and looked at her. "The same. We can't seem to bring the profits up. Eli needs to be booted out, but unfortunately I think I'm the only one that feels that way. And I remain the only female board member, and the youngest by about forty years. You know how that goes."

"Ugh, I'm sorry, hon. That's your parents' legacy there, and those geezers are floating it along like it's a pool noodle. It should be a battleship."

"Agreed, but it's not like I have much help from anyone there with it. You know how it goes. I can bounce ideas off Randall and Dad, but when I bring those ideas back with me the board members all have reasons why they won't work. I mean, some of these guys really need to go. They're ancient. I'm not saying that an older person can't be sharp as a tack, of course. Just not these folks."

"I completely understand. It's the same thing with the zoo sometimes, but at least I have my dad's ear." She stroked the housecat lying on the bed with her. "Yeah, he listens to my ideas and implements at least every third one. They work, but we're still having attendance problems. I guess people just don't go to the zoo anymore. They play video games instead, or something."

"Sorry. But it's good you have George there."

"When can you make it down to Tucson again?"

"School's out at Christmas, and I'm sure I'll need to defrost from the cold weather here."

"Good, because I miss you."

She finished packing, and it was only ten p.m. Not bad. A record, even.

Their flight the next morning was smooth, the whiskey smoother, and the landing the smoothest. Despite her penchant for adventure, Elle really didn't relish flying and was always glad to have a cocktail available to sooth her nerves, though she didn't appreciate Randall giving her *the look* about her screwdriver that morning.

****

First thing Wednesday morning, Michael did something he knew he should do more often. He placed a call to Helen Williams. His mom.

After relaying the events of the past few weeks, he braced himself for the onslaught of questions he was sure she would fire at him regarding Sandra. Surprisingly, there were none. She hadn't even reacted to the news of his engagement being over.

"Elle sounds like a fantastic girl," Helen said. "Don't let her get away."

"I didn't intend to."

"You obviously have some connection with her. Those kinds of things don't happen every day, you know. And you say that she's a widow? What a terrible thing for a young girl to go through. I can't imagine. How is it that she ended up being adopted?"

"Her parents were killed in a car crash when she was just a toddler."

"Oh, how dreadful."

"The Johnstons are good people. It was great of them to take her in. They fit together."

His mom sighed. "Well, I think that this sounds like a new beginning for you. You've started going to the gym again, and you say you haven't had a cigarette in three days? It seems as if she's bringing out some positive change for you."

"Thanks for the encouragement."

"Everything happens for a reason. Now how is that brother of mine doing? Is he up to no good?"

"I'm not exactly sure how to answer that." He stacked and unstacked a pile of coins that sat on his counter.

"I know that tone. He is, isn't he? Ugh. I'm sorry you've gotten mixed up in all that with him. I didn't know. I mean, he's gotten worse the last couple years. I haven't even spoken to him since Christmas. What is he doing?"

He took a deep breath.

"You know what? Never mind. I don't think I want to know. Just tell me it isn't drugs."

"It isn't drugs."

"Ah, that's a relief. Ugh, but now I'm going to wonder what else it could be. Is he embezzling? I'm sorry I asked now."

"Just don't worry, Mom. Try not to. He's been extra busy lately. I'm sure that's why you haven't heard from him. I'll remind him to call you more often." Michael hoped that would satisfy her curiosity.

"I guess that sounds okay. I've got to trust you. Well, if you need anything, anything at all, you know where we are. We love you."

"I love you, too. Thanks."

"And by the way, don't be mad at me, but we never really liked Sandra. She shopped too much."

He couldn't help but laugh. "And that reminds me, I have to call the credit card company today."

"Good luck with that, honey. Keep in touch."

He hung up and stared at the phone, trying to imagine going through life not knowing his flesh and blood parents. He tried to imagine losing a spouse so suddenly, and in such a horrible way. It must have taken a lot for her to trust in him, and he felt very protective of her heart.

On a whim, he ordered a dozen different colored roses to be delivered to her house Friday, knowing they would be waiting for her upon her return. He still had six hours to wait until their plane arrived, and he planned to pick them up personally at the airport. Until then, the day couldn't tick by slower. He filled the minutes with some menial tasks, even playing a few games on his phone, but it didn't make the time go faster and only frustrated him.

When it was finally time to leave for the airport, he left a bit early and got there about a half hour before their flight. Nonetheless, he chanced half-hour parking since it was closer to baggage claim, and if he sat in his car for a while, no one should care.

He checked their flight status on his tablet and seeing their plane had landed on time, he made his way to the end of the passenger hallway near baggage claim.

Michael was a bit surprised to see three bodies approaching him in the terminal, and he was glad for any distraction to keep him from staring at the blonde bombshell coming his way.

He had to keep his cool until he could get her alone and explain himself. Perhaps she felt the same way, after all, she did try to trick him. He shook hands with Randall, and after introductions shook hands with Elizabeth as well. He hugged Elle awkwardly before picking up the women's baggage.

They headed toward his waiting car, and he put their bags in the trunk. Luckily, they'd packed light and it all fit in his Volt. The women took the back seat, and Randall took the passenger seat. The little car sank a few inches closer to the asphalt.

Michael hopped behind the wheel, but before starting the car he turned and shook his finger at Elle.

"Lucy, you have some explaining to do…" he said, in his best impression of Desi Arnaz. Elle gaped, but he continued, "…only because you didn't tell me there were three of you coming, and because I only have three tickets for *Wicked* tonight. So one of us is going to have to sit it out, and it's going to be me." Michael started the car. "Unless I happen to find an extra ticket somewhere, that is. I doubt I will, because it's always sold out."

"Oh no… Sorry," she said.

"It's fine, and I've seen it twice before. Besides, I couldn't get a reservation at Don Antonio's, so I'll take you to the theatre and then put my name on their standby list. That should be enough time for a table to open. I hope everyone is okay with pizza. Theirs is the best in New York."

"That's saying a lot."

As he drove he couldn't help but gaze at her in the rear view mirror each time he stopped at a light. He was really looking forward to seeing the show with them, and struggled to conceal his disappointment. He tried to tell himself it was probably better that he wasn't going. If he went, he'd be tempted to touch her in some way, hold her hand or something, and he couldn't gauge if that would be welcome, especially with other people present. He had no idea if she'd shared anything with them or how she felt about their kiss.

But later that night, when Michael picked them up to take them to the theatre district, he decided it was most definitely best he wasn't going. Elle was utterly stunning in her dress and heels, and with monumental effort, he kept his thoughts and hands to himself, both before the show and afterward when the four of them met up for dinner.

****

Elle wasn't really sure how to interpret Michael's standoffishness that evening, but she caught him watching her numerous times. She guessed he was feeling uncomfortable for having made a pass at her without realizing who she was. Maybe he was angry at the deception, or just embarrassed. After all, professional businessmen don't get involved with their clients, right? Well, he'd had a whole night to think it though, so maybe he'd determined it was best to remain aloof.

She would take his cue. After all, it was nothing. Wasn't it?

The next morning, Randall and Elle met Michael at his office to finalize their business dealings. When they arrived, Michael was still cool and distant. He relayed the news that John had called only minutes before to say that he, unfortunately, could not make the meeting as something "very important" had come up. Elle assumed that was probably why Michael appeared edgy. He assured them that he and his notaries were more than capable of continuing in John Steele's absence. After the necessary formalities, all the relevant documents bore the proper signatures and the surprisingly short and easy meeting drew to a close. Randall was ready to head back to the hotel, but Michael asked Elle to stay behind for a few minutes and wait for him in his office.

So there she sat, staring out at the lower Manhattan skyline, wondering what it was that he wanted to talk about. A picture of an older couple sat on his desk, and she figured it was his parents as there was definitely a family resemblance. She noticed no more personal photos in his office. A lucky bamboo plant on the credenza near the window caught her eye. He seemed to prefer a little messy organization of his paperwork, which sat in a few disheveled heaps on his desk and credenza. She wondered what his place looked like.

The door opened and he came in and shut it behind him. She was surprised he took the chair next to hers instead of sitting behind his desk.

Well, here goes nothing.

"Michael, I never technically lied to you. I don't even know where to begin," Elle said, finally meeting his gaze for a few long moments.

"Oh, do you think I'm upset? No, quite the contrary. I'm impressed."

"Huh?"

"You didn't really think you had me fooled, did you? I knew the first day on the hike that you were the partner. Of course I knew. But it was your game, and I let you play it out."

She stared at him a long while. "Why would you do that?"

"Because I like you, Elle. Which would you rather me call you? Elle or Gabrielle?"

"Elle works." She furrowed her brow, not sure what to make of this conversation. "Is that what you wanted to talk about?"

"Mostly, I wanted to talk about what is happening between us."

Elle looked at the floor. "What about it?" She dreaded his response. Was he going to apologize and tell her they couldn't see each other anymore?

He took her hand. "Look at me. I can't get you out of my head. I need to know, what do you want me to do about this? If you want me to not speak of it again, I will respect that. We'll probably be seeing a lot more of each other in the near future."

She raised her gaze to his, brow still furrowed. "No, no, I don't want that at all. I enjoyed spending the day with you on Sunday. Gosh, was that only a few days ago?"

He released a sigh from deep in his chest, and closed his eyes as if he was offering a silent prayer of thanks. "I'm so glad you feel that way." He stood and pulled her up with him, wrapping his arms around her. "You looked so beautiful last night. I could barely keep myself from touching you."

She leaned back. "Aw, thanks. You looked nice, too."

He stroked her cheek, kissed her gently, and pulled her close again. "So what do you think about a late lunch at…"

The intercom on the phone chimed. "Excuse me,

sorry, I have to take this. It's probably John." He pressed the button. "Yes?"

His receptionist came on the speaker. "Michael, your fiancée is on line two. She says it's an emerg..." He stabbed at the off button with his finger, but didn't hit it quickly enough.

Elle's mouth gaped open. "Fiancée?"

"Just hold on a minute..."

"Fiancée?" she repeated, shrinking away from him.

"Elle, it's not what you think..."

"No. No, it's not. Obviously, we both have secrets." Elle spun on her heel, her eyes welling up, and she fled from Michael's office.

"This can't be happening," Michael said to nobody in particular. He took off after Elle, but she beat him to the elevator, and the door closed right before he reached it.

*****

Elle hit bottom walking and traversed the anonymous streets of New York in a daze. She wasn't sure where she was, where she'd been, or where she was headed.

Fiancée?

The word reverberated in her head like a broken guitar string. It was such a formal word. The precursor to the happiest day in one's life.

She remembered being engaged to Ron, and how proud she had been, happily showing off the ring to everyone and anyone that showed a spark of interest. Planning the wedding, shopping for a dress, setting the registry. She imagined Michael's fiancée was probably doing the same. Perhaps she was sitting at home alone, planning their rehearsal dinner menu and wanted to ask him if he preferred steak or chicken.

Chicken shit!

Weird, though, that he had left his fiancée dangling on the phone and chased her to the elevator. What would he have said to her had she let him explain? Whatever it took to save face, she imagined. Her temples pounded, and she berated herself. She shouldn't have let herself become emotionally involved. That was a ridiculous mistake, and she had become very good at making ridiculous mistakes.

Ridiculous.

The deed was done, the papers were signed. Just because he'd be around Denver didn't mean she'd have to see him. She would make herself scarce.

She shakily wiped her eyes and checked her reflection in a store window. Her cheeks were stained gray with lines of wet mascara, and her eyes were red and puffy. She flipped open her purse, found her travel-sized tissues and blew her nose. After a couple of deep breaths she felt more clear-headed and took out her new cell phone to check her maps app and figure out where she was.

As it happened, she was only a few blocks away from the Macy's flagship store. Elle decided a little retail therapy seemed to be just what the doctor ordered. Or what the doctor would order if there were an adequate doctor nearby.

She called Elizabeth and told her to meet her in the makeup department.

Chapter Ten

Michael's temples pounded. He slammed his office door and tried to figure out how everything seemed to come together and then crumble again so fast. And where the fuck was John? Indeed, Michael had made the excuse for him that morning when he hadn't shown, but this time John hadn't even called, and that wasn't like him.

Michael was more irritated than worried. His uncle was a jerk, but he was an adult and he could take care of himself. But still he was embarrassed as hell that he'd had to make an excuse for John Steele yet again. He was tired of it.

His intercom chimed again, and it was his secretary. "Uh, Michael, John Steele's on the line. And, your fiancée left a message to call her back as soon as possible."

Michael clenched his fists, and said with all the patience he could muster, "She's not my fiancée anymore, Irene. We've been history for weeks."

"Oh? Oh, I didn't know. Michael, I'm sorry…"

"Never mind. Just give me John."

He heard the switch take place, followed by the voice of his uncle. "Hey buddy, you'll never guess where I am."

"You're right, I won't."

"I'm in jail again. Turned out the new girl was a

cop. She's a hot one, too."

"Shit." Michael slumped down in his chair and rubbed his hand over his forehead.

"So you need to get two grand out of the account. That's what they want this time since it's my second arrest."

"Two thousand dollars? Damn." *Shit, damn.*

"And hurry, it stinks in here, and there's some Jew giving me the eyeballs."

"You know, you missed the acquisition meeting this morning. You haven't even asked about it."

"Oh, yeah, yeah, that Denver place. Did they sign it?"

"Yes, and you're lucky they did since you weren't here. The papers are waiting on your desk for your signature before they're filed."

"Great. So hurry up and get me out of here."

Michael didn't respond before hanging up the phone.

Shit, damn.

Michael was of the mindset to let John stew in jail for a while as he'd had just about enough of cleaning up after John's bullshit. John's adequacy to run his company was no longer a question, as he knew beyond a shadow of a doubt that he couldn't.

Michael pondered a long while before an idea struck him, and he strode boldly to John's office. After easily convincing his secretary he needed to see the papers again, he stealthily removed two key pages from the packet. The deal wouldn't be completely legal without them, but no one would notice they were missing unless they were given a reason to look through the mountain of papers. Michael was determined to protect Stone Mountain from his idiot uncle, and at the moment, it was the only way he knew how.

As he made his way back to his office, he passed the break room and grabbed a bag of chips and a soda from the machine. It wasn't a great lunch, but it would do. Besides, he didn't really feel like eating.

He'd wanted to take Elle to a nice Cuban lunch at a place he knew nearby and then head to the Morgan Library. A guard he knew was on duty, and they'd have received a small personal tour. Instead, his afternoon had gone to shit on a shingle. He crunched a chip.

It was mid-afternoon before he finally decided to go to the bank to withdraw the bail money for his uncle, and then he posted it. John was in a foul mood when he was released, but Michael didn't care. His thoughts were elsewhere, on more important things.

Michael took the subway home. He wanted to shower and gather his wits and thoughts before trying to talk to Elle again. He didn't even know if she'd be at the hotel or not. They might be somewhere having dinner. But he had to try. If she wasn't there, he still planned to drive them to the airport the next morning.

He rode the subway back into the city about seven, walked to their hotel and made his way down the hall to room 812. He knocked on the door softly and could hear a TV set on inside. The door opened, still attached to the chain, and he was met with an ice-cold gaze through the slit.

"Can I help you?" Elizabeth asked.

"Elizabeth? It's Michael, and…"

"I know who you are. What do you want?" she asked flatly.

"I need to speak with Elle."

"Who is it?" he heard Elle ask from elsewhere in the room.

"Room service, sweetie, they've got the wrong room," Elizabeth called over her shoulder then brought her cold gaze back to Michael.

"Room service? I didn't order anything." He heard Elle coming toward the door.

"Excuse us," Elizabeth said and shut the door in Michael's face. Michael leaned against the door and heard hushed voices on the other side, but wasn't able to make out what they were saying.

All of a sudden, the door flung open.

"She said she'll talk to you, but if you ever, I mean ever, make her cry again I'm going to shove my foot so far up your ass I'll kick your teeth out. Got it?"

Michael nodded.

The door opened all the way to reveal a pajama- and robe-clad Elle, who was also wearing toe separators with fresh red polish. She carefully waddled out of the room, leaned against the wall opposite Michael, and stared at the floor. Elizabeth shut the door.

"You don't have to do this, Michael. This isn't personal and has nothing to do with us. We already signed the papers, all of that is going forward," she said.

"Will you at least give me a chance to explain everything myself?"

Slowly, her gaze rose to meet his, and he was taken aback by the empty stare. The life that had sparkled behind her blue eyes only a few days ago was gone, and now those eyes were like dull gray stones. He tried to remember the speech he had rehearsed, but suddenly it all seemed…insufficient.

"Well, go on then," she interrupted his train of thought impatiently.

He glanced around. He hadn't planned on doing this in a hotel hallway, but there was a couch at the end of the hall by the elevators, near a floor-to-ceiling window.

"Will you sit with me?" he asked, gesturing toward the couch. Elle didn't answer, but waddled toward the couch. She stood facing the window, looking down at the street below. Michael stood a few steps behind and studied her face in the reflection.

"So how are the wedding plans going?" she asked coldly.

"There isn't going to be a wedding." He saw her close her eyes for a brief second, and then open them again. "It turned out that she was more interested in our real estate agent."

"Meanwhile, you were out trying to have a bit of fun on your own, remember? Sounds like she made the right choice." Elle met his eyes in the window reflection.

He took another step closer, and placed a hand on her shoulder. "Elle, it wasn't like that. She and I were over before that happened."

"Before what happened?" She moved her shoulder so that his hand fell away then turned to face him. "What exactly happened between us? A kiss, that's all. No harm. We're both adults here, right?"

"Elle, let me try to explain everything. I can't go on like this," he pleaded.

She sighed and pursed her lips then turned back to the window, gazing at the street below. There was a bench with an elderly couple sitting on it, holding hands, while they waited for the bus.

"All right," she muttered. "See that bench down there?"

He looked over her shoulder. "Yeah."

"I'll meet you down there. I can't talk to you in my pajamas," she said, then turned to shuffle back to her room without looking at him. He decided to take the stairs to street level to wait for her.

Michael sat on the bench for fifteen minutes, wondering if she would ever come down, and what he would say if she did. The words he had rehearsed for hours seemed not only insufficient, but also hopelessly inadequate.

He glanced at his watch again. Twenty minutes. What took so long? She was probably making him wait on purpose, making him sweat. He supposed, maybe he deserved it, but he resolved to wait all night if he had to.

The city was alive around him. Nameless characters weaved up and down the sidewalk. A vendor hawked gyros from a Greek cart nearby, and the mouth-watering aroma reminded him that he hadn't eaten since breakfast. A gyro would be delicious.

He looked back at the hotel entrance again to see Elle finally walking toward him. She had changed into jeans, a black T-shirt, and sandals. Her hair hung against her face. He stood and walked to meet her. Her jaw was set rigidly when she looked up in greeting.

Finding a quiet place to talk on a busy street in New York City was easier said than done. Michael scanned for a suitable place, but Elle spoke first.

"Look, let's go back inside," she said. "There's a courtyard. It'll be quieter." Before he could reply, she was already heading for the door.

Safely inside the empty, dimly lit courtyard, Michael seated himself on a metal parlor chair across a small table from her. A fountain trickled in the corner as an angelic cherub cheerfully peed into it. Elle folded her hands on the table and stared at them.

Having already discarded all of his previously prepared speeches, he settled on, "Elle, I am so sorry. I never meant to hurt you."

"No, it was my fault. I shouldn't have let my guard down," she said flatly, shaking her head. "All we did was kiss. That isn't a good enough reason for me to be this upset, right? This is so silly. We should just forget it happened and go on with our lives. It was nothing."

"It was much more than that and you know it," he said. He reached for her hand on the table, but she pulled it back and laid it in her lap. "Elle, please, give me another chance. Before I met you, I didn't know it was possible to feel this way about anyone. Whenever I'm around you, I feel like a fool, but you challenge me."

He looked into her stony, gray eyes. "Please give this fool a chance."

He was a broken man needing forgiveness and acceptance, yet she still didn't trust him. She didn't trust anyone at the moment. She inhaled deeply and exhaled slowly, but she listened as he told his story. When he finished, she sat in silence for a long, tense moment, then turned toward Michael and held his hand in hers.

"I don't think now is a good time for either of us," she said, her voice barely audible.

"What do you mean?"

"Look, Sandra hurt you. She betrayed you. Whether you think it does or not, it matters because it only happened a few weeks ago."

"A month."

"Okay, a month. Still, you were with her for three years. Three years. That's a very long time."

"I'm over her." Michael straightened up.

Elle sighed. "I understand you are trying to be honest about what you think you feel…"

"What I *think* I feel?"

"Please let me finish. I think we need to keep our distance for a while. It would make me feel much better to know you've had some time to heal first."

"My heart was numb to her a long time ago."

Elle cocked her head to the side at him. "Then why didn't you break it off a long time ago? Why do you still get rigid in your jaw when you talk about her? It's still fresh, Michael. She tore your heart out, didn't she? I don't want to be your rebound girl. I deserve more, and so do you."

Michael let out a long breath and spoke again, low. "You are right. I do have lots of anger in my heart right now, and your argument makes sense. I can't love you right while I hold anger in the same space."

Love?

Elle nodded. "I'm glad you understand. I have to go now."

"Let me walk you up," he offered.

"No, just let me go," she said, her voice cracking.

When Elle stood, she avoided his gaze, moved out of his grasp and quickly walked away.

Michael glanced over his shoulder at the little cherub fountain. The peeing angel smiled back at him as the color changing LEDs in the water cycled through the rainbow. He made a mental note never to book clients at this particular hotel again. It was tacky.

He also knew he wasn't going to let Elle get away. She was good for him. She could see inside of him better than he ever could. Infinitely better than Sandra ever could. And, if Elle could see him, truly *see* him, she was the *one* for him. He only hoped he could eventually be the *one* for her as well.

Chapter Eleven

Michael took the N train home. He liked the subway. It was always so…efficient. If it broke down or service was interrupted, the problem only lasted a relatively short time. Yet, other riders always seemed annoyed at the inconvenience.

First-world problems.

He idly wished he could make the first-world people understand things like on-time arrival statistics for each train, and the extreme rarity of service interruptions, but of course he knew it was a lost cause. People tended to live in their own bubbles, without seeing the bigger picture most of the time.

For most people, there is no big picture. Their own little picture is as big as it gets.

Fortunately, there were no service interruptions on the train that night. As it pulled under the Queensboro Bridge, Michael looked around at the few other passengers. A nice-looking couple sat close by, holding hands, she with her head on his shoulder and a take-out box in her lap. A young hipster male glared at the newspaper, angrily turning the pages. An elderly woman, arms crossed, stared at the floor. Above her head was the common public service sign advising everyone: *If you see something, say something.*

He took a breath and leaned his head back.

I did. I saw her and I told her.

The train emerged from the tunnel and lurched to a stop, but it wasn't his stop yet. No one got off or on the train. The doors closed and it moved forward again, around the wide, bumpy turn into Queens.

Michael stopped at the twenty-four-hour market on the corner near his station to get a bag of chips and a beer. It was one a.m. when he unlocked his door, but he was wide-awake, tense and antsy. He fired up his laptop and had just started to purge e-mails when something that had been lurking at the back of his mind suddenly rushed front and center. He crunched away at greasy potato chips, and stared at his laptop.

No more service interruptions. It's time to arrive at something.

Michael began his second Internet investigation of Elle Johnston.

And in less than one second, Google gave him over a million hits. She did have a very common name. Not good enough. It was time to narrow the field down a bit more. He ate a few chips and typed "Jake Johnston, Denver" into the search engine. Over two million hits this time. But some determined prowling on business networking sites yielded results. Michael clicked to open a window and skimmed the pages until he found the Jake Johnston that lived in Denver.

"Stone Mountain Partners... Blah, blah, blah..." Michael knew all that already. He skimmed through more biographies, now looking for references to San Diego. And eventually, as his eyes scanned the bottom of one particular page, he dropped a chip into his lap.

Jake Johnston, Operations Manager, Duncan Land Development. San Diego, California.

"There you are," he said aloud to no one. He

bookmarked the page and entered "Duncan Land Development" in the search window. Not surprisingly, a link for Duncan Land Development appeared at the top of the list. Their website showcased several retail properties, a shopping mall, condominium complexes and a high rise in downtown San Diego. He clicked on the link Business History.

"With over forty years' experience... Yeah." He scrolled down and found an old color photograph, under which the name "William Duncan" was typed. There was a definite resemblance. William had a kindly face, and Elle had her father's blue eyes.

"Well, hello there, Mr. Duncan. Nice to meet you."

Michael opened another browser window and entered "William Duncan San Diego." And this time, after less intense browsing, he found a reference to an article in the archives of a San Diego business magazine. After double-clicking, the computer screen froze. He let out a groan of frustration waiting for the page to load.

The article finally loaded, and he printed it for fear the computer might decide to lock up on him again. The headline announced, "William Duncan's 21-year-old daughter takes her place among the Board of Directors at Duncan Land Development."

He got up, grabbed his beer, took a long drink and sat down to read the page.

"William Duncan's only daughter and heir, Gabrielle, joined the Board of Directors of Duncan Land Development at their annual meeting in San Francisco last week. Later, she toured some of the company's San Diego ventures and attended a small press conference held at the Coronado Hotel. When asked how she felt about joining the company, Elle answered: 'My father founded this company and built it from the ground up. I am very proud of what he accomplished, and I am very proud of the team that has managed it since his death. I am honored to be a part of that team now, and I thank them for their dedication throughout the years…'"

Michael leaned back in the chair and read through to the end of the article. He switched to the company's website again and clicked on the link for "Board Members."

Oddly, she wasn't listed. Had she resigned? Why would she do that?

He typed "Duncan Land Development SEC filings" into the search engine. Under the 14-A form for Board Member Compensation from two years previous, Michael scanned for Gabrielle and nearly fell off his chair. He re-counted the zeros with his finger following along on the screen just to be sure he was seeing straight. Indeed, there were five of them. She had made two hundred grand that year, and it didn't include whatever she might have inherited. Yet, she lived in such a modest house…

A few hundred questions pinballed through his mind, but the loudest one was *WHY?*

It was late, and he still didn't feel tired. He entered "Elle Johnston" and clicked on images. He had been down this track before, and in no time at all there she was. A few pictures of her popped up from social networking sites. Generally, Michael had no interest in these. He figured everyone he wanted to talk to was already in touch with him, but it was easy to join. Maybe he could link up with her online and have some small connection.

If she'd accept me, that is.

He paged through a desktop folder of personal photos until he found something suitable for his profile picture. To his surprise, after he signed up, a few familiar names instantly popped up as friend suggestions. It was almost creepy.

Elle was easy to find, and he'd found her before, but not on the service itself. He wasn't able to see anything on her page, and he didn't understand why. After all, he could click on other people's pages and see far more than anyone could ever give a shit about. Maybe she hadn't been on in a long time? Or maybe he was overly tired and needed to figure the site out when he was well rested.

It was already two-thirty in the morning, and he had been up for over twenty hours. It was way past time for bed and when his head hit the pillow, he fell asleep almost instantly.

****

Elle knew she wouldn't be sleeping well at all that night. Her mind swam with unpleasant images from the evening's confrontation: Michael explaining his ex-fiancée situation, the little angel peeing into a giant bucket...

"What was that all about?" Elizabeth asked Elle when she returned to the room.

"Ugh, nothing. I don't want to talk about it. What's for dinner?"

"You sure you don't want to talk about it?" Elizabeth stroked her arm in a comforting gesture.

Elle nodded.

"Well, okay then. Randall called from his room. He

wants to meet up in the lobby and go down to Times Square. I bet we can find something to eat there."

"Sounds fun," Elle said, but she didn't mean it. She wasn't hungry, and that was rare for her. She usually had quite the healthy appetite, and New York food was divine. But tonight she had no interest in dinner. None at all. Wine...yes. Bring on the wine.

Ten minutes later, they were in a cab headed for Times Square. The driver dropped them off at the east end so they could walk up to where the Red Stairs were.

Each of the three had been to New York at least a few times before, but not so many times that Times Square had lost its novelty. Still, Elle's mood was less than festive, and she could barely tolerate the crowd. Randall steered them into a giant toy store, and promptly went in search of some souvenirs for the children at home. Elle and Elizabeth got caught up in the Barbie doll section, reminiscing a little about their childhood favorites. It took a long time for Randall to find them, but he was ready to leave, bag in hand.

"We need to find some food," he said. "I'm *hangry*. You know what that means, right? I'm so hungry I'm angry!" He crossed his eyes and grimaced for emphasis.

"Me, too, but not the hungry part," Elle answered under her breath. Was she angry? No, not really. Just numb. She needed that glass of wine.

They bravely entered into the flow of human foot traffic, like three small corpuscles entering a major artery of the huge beast that was Manhattan. Randall spotted a McDonalds, and the line didn't seem particularly long, but the women vetoed the idea. About a block away was a nice restaurant, but none of them were thrilled with the prospect of a two-hour wait.

They settled for a chain Italian restaurant at the end of the street and a twenty-minute wait. They were a bit disheartened to end up at a restaurant they could all find in their own hometowns, but at least the view was spectacular.

Hours later, when Elle was finally drifting off, her final thoughts were of Michael. She really hoped he would keep his word and get his life back together, not only for his sake but also because she wanted another chance with him. She knew she would see him in the morning, as he was their ride to the airport. She would have to steel her nerves to make it through that ride without breaking.

And she would. She had survived worse.

Chapter Twelve

Michael's alarm announced it was five thirty a.m. and he groaned. He'd not slept well for the last two hours he'd been in bed, tossing and turning the whole time because he knew he had to get up early to drive into the city to retrieve Elle, Randall, and Elizabeth from the hotel and deposit them at the airport as he'd promised.

Sure, he could have arranged a car service, but he always felt personal service was always a better touch in business dealings. Besides, he was beyond curious to gauge Elle's reaction to him that morning.

He showered, dressed, ate a bowl of Irish oatmeal and grabbed his keys to head out.

As he was driving, his cell phone rang. He knew he shouldn't answer while driving, but he did because he didn't recognize the number. It could be Elle.

"Hi Michael," he heard Sandra say.

"Good-bye."

"Wait! Wait, please!"

"What?"

"I really need to talk to you. Can you please meet with me today?" she pleaded.

He sighed. "Look, whatever you have to say, say it now. And quick, I'm driving."

"It's a little more complicated than that. I'd really rather talk about it in person. It's your choice of where and when. I'm completely at your disposal."

He stopped at a light, watching a mom and daughter cross the street, holding hands. "All right. I'm dropping some clients off at JFK this morning. I can meet you at the diner on Thirty-third at say, one?"

"Okay, and thank you."

He hung up and continued through the tunnel into Manhattan. Over the last few years he'd become excellent at navigating the streets, and he actually liked driving in the city. Most people absolutely hated it, but he welcomed the challenge. He was only one of a few people he knew that even had a car.

When he arrived at the hotel, his passengers were already waiting on the curb for him, just as planned. Elle was pleasant enough, but he could tell she had a wall up when her smile didn't reach her eyes. He resisted the urge to apologize again, reasoning he didn't want to come off as too desperate, even if he was. No one liked a desperate man.

After saying good-byes at the airport, he realized it was already almost time to meet Sandra. He knew he'd probably get there a bit early, but that was okay because he'd already installed the social networking app on his phone and was kind of looking forward to playing with it.

He parked the Volt in his own driveway then walked the couple blocks to the diner. As he rounded the corner he was surprised to see that Sandra was already there. She sat at an outside table, her back to him, the sun glinting off her shiny, shoulder-length brown hair. Her hands were folded in front of her and her head was lowered, he presumed she was checking her cell phone.

He was somewhat alarmed to not feel the urge to turn around and leave at the sight of her. Instead, he walked to her and she turned. Her face was shrouded with a worry he'd never seen, and she forced a smile.

"Hello Sandra," he said, taking the chair across from her. He scooted it in and nodded.

She placed her phone face down on the table, folded her hands and took a breath. "Thanks for showing up."

"Sure. So what's up?"

"Well..." She took another breath. He really wanted her to just get on with it, but a waiter interrupted, setting a glass of water in front of him and handing him a menu.

"No thanks, I won't be staying for lunch." He waved it off.

"Very well, sir."

Sandra appeared a bit dejected at that, but still smiled pleasantly. "Must be a busy day at the office," she said.

He nodded and took a sip of water.

"I needed to talk to you because I was laid off from work. They had a big cut yesterday. They let six of us go."

There it was. She was looking for money. "Oh, I'm sorry to hear that. Truly. You've been there awhile. Can you apply for unemployment?"

"Yes, they gave me the information, and I'm checking into it. But there's something else..."

"Yes?"

"I'm not really sure how to say this so I guess I'll just...I'm pregnant."

His heart sank like a boulder, then he realized that

there was no way it was his as they hadn't had sex for at least four months. He added it all up while his eyes traveled down to her belly.

"Don't worry, it's not yours. It's Mark's."

He released the breath he didn't realize he was holding in. "Umm…"

"I'm only about a month and a half along. No one knows yet."

"Okay, but Mark knows, right?" He hoped to God that she hadn't chosen to tell him first instead of the father.

"He knows. I told him two days ago. That's when I went to my doctor and found out for sure."

"And…?" He could tell by her expression that the news must not have gone over as well as she'd hoped.

"Well, of course he assured me that he'd take care of us."

"That's good, then. Did your work know?"

"No, and there's nothing that can be done now. Perhaps I wouldn't have gotten laid off if I'd told them, but I wanted to wait a bit first."

"Doesn't matter now."

"And I don't know about Mark. I don't know what's going to happen. He didn't seem to be too happy about it and he's been very distant." Her voice broke and she started to cry. She lowered her head to her hands. "What have I done? I've completely messed up my life now."

Michael felt beyond awkward. How was he supposed to comfort the woman who'd cheated on him and was now pregnant with the other man's child? If he hadn't walked in on them, he wondered if she would have figured out a way to make him think that the baby was his.

"I'm so sorry," she murmured between sobs.

Other diners were looking, so he stroked her arm. "I'm sure everything will work out okay. He said he'd take care of you."

"Yes, he did. But I didn't want it to be this way. No, I didn't want it to be such a crappy situation."

"Do you doubt him?"

"Yes."

Michael leaned back in his chair. So she had decided to cheat on him with someone she didn't even fully trust? Comforting.

"What is it that you need from me? Why did you want to see me today?"

She raised her gaze to his. "I'm truly sorry for everything I've put you through. I know, we aren't meant to be together, I realize that now. I'm not asking for that, I don't want that. I'm not asking for your forgiveness either, but I do want to earn it. I'm asking for you to not give up on me. I don't have many people to rely on, you know that, and I've made some huge mistakes. This little baby"—she rubbed her belly— "this baby is a blessing and a new beginning for me. I want to be a good mommy for him, or her."

"I understand that," he said, but what could he do for her? What was he prepared to do for her?

"Also, I want to pay off the debt I've incurred for you as well. Eventually."

Wow, she seemed serious. Nonetheless, his head throbbed. He ran his hands through his hair.

"I'm wondering if you know anyone who's hiring right now?" she asked.

"I can't think of anyone, but I'll let you know if I

hear of anything. Definitely."

"Thank you. Really, your kindness means a lot."

"You're welcome." His mind was still reeling over all the new information, plus he was also trying to remember if anyone he knew had an opening for someone with her qualifications.

"I'm glad you decided to meet me. I was afraid you wouldn't," she said. "I'm just...I'm really, really sorry."

The waiter appeared and placed a chopped salad in front of her, dressing on the side, and a small bread basket with butter.

She buttered a roll, took a bit and asked, "What about Steele? Do you guy need a runner or an office clerk?"

He thought about it. "We might, let me ask around."

"Thank you, I would really appreciate that."

The waiter appeared to inquire of her satisfaction with the meal.

"You know what, go ahead and bring me a menu. I think I'll have something after all," he directed the waiter.

"Right away, sir."

Sandra smiled.

Chapter Thirteen

Elle got home to Denver late in the evening and was surprised to find a note from her neighbor pasted on her door.

Please come over right away, no matter the time.

She pulled her carry-on into her living room, patted George on the head, and then went next door.

Betty met her at the door. "I'm sorry, I tried to keep them alive, but I think they might have already been out in the sun too long. Damn delivery guy, what an idiot. He shouldn't have left them out there like that." She led Elle through her house to the kitchen.

She was an adorable lady with curly white hair and an amazing green thumb for growing just about anything she planted in her yard. Elle adored her and wished she could grow her own garden as well.

On her kitchen counter sat a large, lovely, yet somewhat wilted bouquet of multicolored roses.

"I didn't open the card. I knew you were going to be out today, because it's Friday and you have school, so I can't imagine who they came from." Betty winked. It was clear to Elle that she was expecting her to open the card right away. She would placate Betty's friendly curiosity; besides, Elle already had a suspicion of where they came from.

She was right.

Betty tiptoed and tried to read over her shoulder.

117

"They're from a guy that works with Randall," Elle said, tucking the card back in the envelope. "Thanks for taking care of them."

"Do you like him?" Betty inquired.

"Yeah, he's okay. We're friends."

"Friends don't send roses, honey. Friends send daisies."

Elle smiled. "Betty, he's a business partner. There's nothing going on there."

"Yet you seem wistful."

"I'm tired from flying."

"Flying? Where were you?"

"New York. We just got back from signing the acquisition papers yesterday morning."

"Wow, I wasn't aware that you and Randall were in financial trouble. You know, I have a little money tucked away. I could loan you some if you ever need it. I don't have family, who's it going to go to anyways? My dog, little foot humper that he is?"

"That's not necessary, but I appreciate the offer."

"You want a cup of tea while you're here?"

"Sure."

Elle needed the break, and she appreciated the concern Betty showed. It felt nice to have someone care.

Later, she hefted the half-wilted bouquet into her house and sat it on the kitchen counter. She removed the roses, separated the baby's breath filler, snipped the shriveled leaves off the stems, and arranged the roses into a smaller vase. Hopefully, they'd perk up again.

She removed her painting from above her fireplace mantel, placed the bouquet in the place of honor, and then sank into her fluffy white sofa and contemplated the cheerfully colored blooms. It had been years since she'd received flowers, and honestly, she'd never seen a bouquet so big or so beautiful. Multi-colored roses were a very nice and unexpected touch.

She read his card again. All it said was: *Have a great day. Michael.* Yep, that's all it said, typed out by the floral company no doubt, and she really couldn't be certain how to take it.

Her phone rang.

It was Elizabeth calling from the airport to chat while she waited for her connecting flight back to Tucson, which was delayed. After chatting with her friend for a bit, mostly keeping her entertained while she waited, Elle said her good-byes and headed to the kitchen.

Nothing looked particularly appetizing in her fridge, and she wondered what Betty might have sitting in hers. She entertained the notion to go find out when a bottle of pink moscato caught her eye that she'd had for a while. Tonight seemed like the right night to open it. She sat it on the counter to let it breathe for a few minutes while she put the clean dishes away and fed George. She took a glass down from the cupboard and grasped the bottle to pour, but the condensation made it too slippery to hold, and it clattered to the floor with a neat crack. The sweet pink wine quickly spilled across her tile and spread under the fridge.

"Hello?" she called upon entering their front door, happy to be home from a four-day trip to San Diego. Ron was in his fourth week of chemotherapy, and she hadn't wanted to go to the trip, but he'd insisted he was fine. Were all men so stubborn as the ones in her life?

"Hey babe, can you grab the moscato out of the

fridge?" he answered, from the bedroom. Of course, he wasn't supposed to have wine while on the chemotherapy, but a sip wouldn't hurt.

Elle set down her bags and took two wineglasses out of the cabinet. She was just pulling the wine out of the fridge when Ron cleared his throat behind her.

He was wrapped in a towel, and he was…bald.

She dropped the wine.

Elle cursed and kneeled to retrieve the broken bits of glass. She put them in the garbage can, then headed to the hall closet to retrieve a towel to soak up the mess.

After laying the towel out over the spill, she prodded at it with her foot to soak up some more liquid.

"Yeah, the towel is new. What do you think? Is it my color?" Ron turned from side to side like a model in an attempt to distract her from the obvious change.

"Your…hair," she managed to whisper, hoarsely.

The bottle gently rolled to its side. Luckily it hadn't shattered.

"I figured it would happen soon enough, and I already had some clumps that came out in the shower a few times. Why hold it off, you know? It feels good, actually. I don't think I've been this bald since the day I was born." He rubbed his bald head with one palm, still holding the towel with the other.

She couldn't help the tears welling up in her eyes. Ron had always prided himself in his long, shiny, dark brown hair. When she met him, he kept a few dreadlocks in it. Then, when he moved to Denver with her, he'd removed the locks and trimmed it to a more reasonable length…a length more suitable for a white water rafting guide.

The first towel soaked through. Elle retrieved a

second one and pulled the fridge away from the wall.

"Does it really? Feel better, I mean?" she asked hopefully.

Ron's eyes glistened as he shook his head. She wrapped her arms around him.

"No, love," he said. "Actually, it feels awful."

Elle cleared the rest of the liquid, and then retrieved the mop to finish the job. Tears filled her eyes, but she was thankful to have the current task of cleaning to distract her from her memories. When she was done, she sat on the kitchen floor. Food didn't sound good, wine sounded worse now, and sleep wasn't going to happen for a while.

George came in and dusted her nose with his tail.

When they were married, Ron understood when she'd expressed her desire of keeping her adoptive name instead of taking his. When Ron passed away, she regretted her decision. A little over a year later, Jake was diagnosed with cancer, and when he retired, he transferred ownership of SMP to Randall and Gabrielle Johnston. It was actually a good thing she hadn't changed her name, as the paperwork would have been a headache.

She decided a bath was in order. Since the master bedroom only had a shower—something she'd always wanted to change about the house. She toted her bathing essentials to the spare bathroom, which was equipped with a tub and shower combo. As the tub filled, she opened the medicine cabinet to see if she'd placed some bath salts in there.

The sight of Ron's bathroom items brought her pause. She took out his toothbrush and reverently sat it on the counter, followed by his other necessities. Last, she brought out his bottle of Pasha. She removed the lid and sniffed the spray opening, her mind filling with a hundred memories. Tears clouded her eyes as she inhaled again.

After arranging his toiletries on the counter, she settled into the bath and set the bottle of cologne on the rim of the tub, contemplating it. Tears flowed freely down her face and she was somewhat surprised at the depth of emotion she felt. She wept with abandon like she hadn't since his death.

She wasn't over Ron and never would be. He was stolen from her too fast, and they didn't get to have their life together. The same with her parents. It was all so unfair and sometimes she felt completely and utterly alone.

George wandered in to sit on the bathmat and stare at her. She expected him to hop on the rim of the tub and drink the water like he usually did, but he didn't. He jumped up on the counter and sniffed Ron's belongings, then rubbed his neck on them gently, while purring the loudest she'd ever heard him purr.

Perhaps she needed to take her own advice, the advice that she'd given Michael, and let herself heal. She hadn't been aware of how much pain she'd been holding in.

She resolved to go to her spot on the mountain ledge the next day and officially say good-bye to Ron.

****

Friday afternoon, Michael was surprised to receive a call from Patrick, a fellow employee at the firm, asking him to meet up for cocktails. He said it was important. Patrick lived in Queens as well, so they picked a place they were both familiar with.

After finishing early at the office, Michael headed home to regroup, then to the bar. It had been an all-around shitty week, full of ups and downs, and he was in major need of a reset and a cold beer. The bar was moderately full, mostly of young professionals, but it wasn't packed yet. It would certainly become busier and louder as the night wore on. He ordered at the counter, and then found a table near the rear of the room. Patrick showed up a few minutes later, easily recognizable by his extremely tight, dark curls. It almost looked like he had a perm right out of the seventies.

"Hey man, haven't seen you for a few weeks. How are you?" he asked, stretching out his hand.

"I'm good, how have you been?" Patrick answered. He must have come straight from the office since he still wore his messenger bag, which he removed and sat on the table. Michael had never followed the trend of wearing a "man purse," instead opting to carry a backpack, which he usually slung over one shoulder.

"You ordering?" Michael asked.

"Yeah, give me a second," Patrick said, and went to the counter. He returned, reverently carrying a tall beer as if it were of utmost importance. Michael realized perhaps Patrick had had just as shitty of a week as he'd had.

"How's it going, Mike?" Patrick asked.

"It's all fucked up!" Michael exclaimed, using a sarcastic expression they used often when they worked together on a project, especially if the project was going well.

"I heard about Denver. Well done, my friend, well done."

"And how's Cincinnati?" Michael asked, referring to Patrick's current project.

"Going really well," he answered, which meant it wasn't.

"Sorry to hear. Is that what you want to discuss?"

"Your uncle John is a fucking asshole!"

Michael laughed. "Well, why don't you tell me exactly how you feel about him?"

Patrick laughed as well. "I mean, seriously! Hookers again? Jesus! What would happen if someone found out? A client or the press? I know he's family and all, but we need to do something about him. He's too risky."

"I completely agree, but what do you suggest?"

"A few of us think you should take his place."

Michael swallowed hard.

"I mean, we know he's your uncle and all—"

"I have no love for him."

"—and we feel that you are fit for the position. You've proven yourself time and again. We need to figure out how to get him out. How do you feel about that?" Patrick asked.

Michael took a sip of his beer. "*We* whom?"

A waiter arrived with Michael's nachos and a slice of pizza for Patrick.

"We as in all of us junior execs including myself, Todd, Pam, and Rodney. They're all either out on a call or busy tonight; otherwise, they'd be here. Oh, but Pam said we could call her if you want."

"Maybe in a bit. What are we going to do? Have you thought of a plan?" Michael was conscious to leave out the fact that he did own the controlling share of their stocks. Or at least he could own them in a matter of days if he ever needed to.

"That depends. Are you willing to step up?"

"What about you?"

Patrick laughed. "Me? You've worked there longer."

"Yeah, but you have a better track record. And honestly, I'm not certain I want to be the boss. I like what I do, and I'd like it better if I was working for a better person. I think that better person could be you, and I agree. John needs to go. He's an embarrassment. He didn't even show up for my acquisition yesterday morning because he was in jail again, as you've no doubt heard. We need to figure out how to fairly oust him, or get him to resign on his own. It would look better, and we want to keep our hands clean."

"Understood," Patrick said. "Thank you for the vote of confidence, but you're the man. As long as we're on the same page right now, we'll turn it when it's the right time."

****

The next morning, Elle rose with the sun again. She dressed in her most comfortable hiking pants, a good pair of shoes, a shirt, and then tied her hair in a scarf.

With tears, she methodically packed John's last belongings into a box, leaving the Pasha bottle out, and carefully closed the lid. She carried the box to her Jeep and placed it on the floor of the passenger's side.

She came back in and ate a bowl of cereal and an apple. She then filled her hydration pack and brought that to her Jeep as well. Last, she pulled Ron's mountain bike off its holder in her garage and attached it to the back of her Jeep.

Everything was packed and ready, only she wasn't. She knew she never would be, but it had to be done. It was time for her to move on. She'd already grieved for him for two years.

As the sun began to warm the day, Elle started her Jeep and pulled onto the freeway, headed to her sanctuary in the mountains to say good-bye to the man she loved.

She was glad to see there were few other cars parked in the gravely lot at the trailhead. As the air grew crisper, closer to fall, the hikers became sparse. Elle left the box and bike with the Jeep, but brought the bottle of cologne with her.

She traversed the trail, easily reaching the point where her rock cliff was, the point where she and Michael had stood only a few weeks previous. The sweeping view of the valley below always took her breath away and today was no exception. The stone was cold when she sat on it. She removed the cologne bottle from her pack, sniffed it, and let the memories flood into her mind, just as the sweet pink wine had flooded her kitchen floor so swiftly the night before, igniting the moment. She sprayed the cologne into the air and watched a shimmering cloud of droplets drift off the edge of the ledge.

Perhaps she should say something aloud, or do something special to mark the occasion but she couldn't really think of anything. She continued to let the memories come as they did, and let the tears flow however they would. Sometimes a formal good-bye could not work; it had to be organic.

An organic good-bye would be fitting for her carefree, wild-haired husband. She remembered the first time she'd seen him on the beach, rising out of the ocean with his surfboard like some god. In all her twenty-one years, she'd never seen a more perfect specimen of man, and with such gorgeous hair. She was hooked on his gentle, wild soul from day one and had fallen in love headfirst.

But now that soul was gone, and she'd never look into his loving green eyes again. In the end, she'd been the fearful one, and he'd been brave. She wished she could turn back the clock and relive all of their moments over again, but knew she couldn't.

Ron used to say "today is a gift, that's why it's called the present." She knew it was cliché, so she usually smiled and didn't think of the deeper meaning of his words. But today she did, and the pain was fresh and acute. Never again would she take a day for granted.

Finally feeling purged, she sprayed one last spritz of his cologne, watching the shimmering droplets float over the ledge. Just then, a large hawk swept up majestically from below, and climbed high into the sky, circling wide and proud. The air was so still she could clearly hear the whip of his strong wings beating like a heart. She watched the hawk until it disappeared from view, too far away to see any longer, but still flying high and free.

"Good-bye, Ron. I loved you." She wiped the last of the tears from her eyes.

On the way home from the mountain that day, she stopped in a shopping center and donated the box and bike to a Goodwill donation truck stationed there.

She did decide to keep three things, though…the cologne, Monstro, and his voice on her house number voicemail. Heck, no one ever used the house number anymore besides her. She still liked to call at least once every few days to hear his voice.

****

The next month whizzed by surprisingly fast and uneventful since John Steele seemed to be minding his manners. Perhaps he sensed his employees hated him. Or—and it was an extremely low possibility—he might have decided to actually attempt to be a better person all around.

Unlikely.

Nonetheless, Michael kept his finger on the pulse of Steele, waiting for any sign that he'd have to play either of the two cards he held—the papers that would protect Stone Mountain from being sold again, and the stock that his mother held.

Michael spent more and more time in Denver, going over new policies and procedures with Randall and the employees, and streamlining their business. And, thanks to a referral from an old college buddy, he had rented an apartment not far from the firm. No more hotel rooms. Plus, it felt good to be back in his hometown, especially now that he saw it in a completely new light. He often stared at the mountains in the distance and wondered why he hadn't explored them more when he was younger.

He hadn't seen Elle, or heard from her since the morning he'd dropped her off at JFK. But he knew she was fine, as Randall would certainly have let him know otherwise. On a whim, he decided to give her a call one day when he was headed back to New York.

"Hi, it's Ron," said a male voice on the voicemail, followed by Elle's voice echoing a cheerful, "And

Elle!" The male voice started again, "We're off on an adventure right now, so leave a message and"—then both voices together—"we'll call you back!" *Beep*.

Michael hung up without leaving a message and slumped farther into the airport chair.

As he boarded the plane, he felt a tangible pain in his heart when his foot left the ramp.

The seat he was assigned was near the window, and he leaned against it, staring at the beautiful snowcapped mountains in the distance. They were Elle's refuge, her sanctuary. He felt as if they were glaring at him.

After the plane took off, its flight path circled over the section of town where Elle lived. Michael held his hand against the glass and bid her a silent good-bye, then leaned back in the seat and closed his eyes, trying to organize his jumbled thoughts. The only thing he knew for certain was that Elle's face still topped every list in his mind, and he would find a way to make things right. The wounded look in her eyes when she backed away from him that day was one he never wanted to see again.

His cell phone buzzed as he unlocked the door to his New York apartment when he got home that evening. He could barely push the door open because of the pile of junk mail and catalogues on the floor.

When he finally took his phone out of his pocket and checked it, he smiled.

"Halloween party—my house. Oct. 24, 9pm 'til whenever. She'll be there. Randall."

Chapter Fourteen

The blaring music gave Elle a bit of a headache, as she hadn't gotten much sleep in the past few days due to an annoying case of insomnia named "Michael is in town." She knew he was going to be attending Randall's annual Halloween party, but so far she hadn't seen him, and her nerves were shot.

Tom leaned over and spoke loudly close to her ear, "I gotta take a huge piss!"

"Ugh, thanks for the info, friend."

Elle had agreed to attend the party with Tom as friends, nothing more. Heck, she'd known him almost as long as she'd known Randall and the thought of being anything more than just his friend made her nauseous, and she knew it did him as well. Nonetheless, they came to the party together dressed as a vampire and his victim.

When he'd shown up at her door, she realized they should have shopped for their costumes together, as they didn't exactly match. He was wearing jeans and his motorcycle jacket, and she was in a somewhat Victorian-looking dress with lace up boots. She wore a long prosthetic gash in her neck, complete with dried stage blood that ran down her cleavage in two dainty ribbons.

Biker-vamp Tom hadn't shopped for much except fangs and a stick-on mustache. He'd already lost the fangs somewhere, but he still wore the mustache. She didn't fully understand his thought process on why a vampire would sport a mustache.

Elle weaved her way in the opposite direction of Tom, escaping through the patio into the cool night air and was glad the old black dress had long sleeves. The plunging neckline was a bit chilly, but she wasn't planning to stay out long; just take a few breaths, refocus, and then slip back inside where it was warm. She walked to the edge of the patio and looked up at the big, full moon that smiled back at her.

Happy Halloween, moon.

A hand reached around her, holding a glass.

"I thought red wine was appropriate."

She didn't have to turn to know who it was, and her heart leaped. "Michael. I didn't know you were going to be here tonight," she lied. She took the glass and swirled the liquid around, watching it.

"I got here about half an hour ago."

"And it took you this long to find me?"

"No, I saw you the minute I came in. I wanted a good look at you in case you decided to leave once you saw me."

Elle turned to face him. He was dressed as a doctor with a white lab coat, a wild gray-haired wig, and a stethoscope around his neck.

He bit his lip and looked at her neck with mock concern. "That's a terrible looking wound, my dear. You might need stitches. I should examine it closer in some better light." He ran his finger down the side of her neck. "Yes, I think you're going to need a thorough examination."

"I don't think my date would appreciate that," Elle

answered, suddenly feeling warm despite the chill outside. Her nipples hardened. She focused on the embroidered name across the breast pocket of his lab coat.

"Dr. Phil Good?" She couldn't help but snicker when she read it out loud.

"I know, goofy, huh? But it's all I could find." He shrugged. "And what's this about a date?"

"I came with Tom."

"Is he aware you're on a date together?"

"Of course he is. Why?"

Michael nodded toward the house. Elle followed his gaze to the window and saw Tom dancing with two women, both dressed as Little Bo Peep. One of them smacked him on the rear with her staff.

"Well, I'm sure you knew I was lying," she said with a chuckle.

"Yes. But there's one thing I don't know yet. What are your plans next weekend?"

"I'll probably go trick-or-treating with the niece and nephew. Why?"

"I happen to have an extra ticket for the Living Dead show on Friday. I remember you were playing them in your Jeep. Oh, excuse me. Monstro."

"What?" Elle couldn't help but let her excitement show. She remained adolescent about some things, and music was one of them. "But they're not going to be here next weekend. I haven't heard anything advertised."

"You're correct. They'll be in New York, but that's okay." He shrugged. "I have plenty of friends that might be interested in going backstage, if you don't want to come."

"Backstage? How did you manage that?"

"I've got connections. Does it matter? Are you coming with me?"

"It sounds like you are trying to bribe me."

"Shamelessly. I am, yes."

She cleared her throat and tried unsuccessfully to hold back a smile as she said, "Yes."

"Mmm." He nodded thoughtfully, studying her. "Come on; let's get your sexy dead body back inside where it's warm."

He led her inside where the rhythmic bass of a dance tune thumped so loud it made her bones tickle. The Johnstons' large living room played double duty as a dance floor for parties when all of the furniture had been moved out. Randall was lucky to have a neighbor who deejayed on the weekends and was glad to help out for a party. The dark lighting with the green and blue bulbs gave the room an eerie appearance of a zombie prom.

Michael pulled Elle close to him and began to dance with her. She hesitated at first, then matched his movements. Feeling his body so close to hers was exhilarating. She turned around and leaned her back against him, moving with the music and losing herself in it.

"I have to go down the hall," she whispered in his ear during the lull of a song change.

"Let me get you another glass of wine," he offered and they went separate ways.

When she exited the bathroom, he was standing right there and pushed her back in. He closed the door behind him and set her glass on the counter.

"What are you doing?" She giggled.

"I told you, I have to have a look at this wound."

"All right, Doctor." With mock obedience, she pushed her hair out of the way and tilted her head.

"Nope, up here you go." He picked her up and sat her on the counter. "There, that's better. What kind of horrible creature would do this to you?"

Tipsy, she giggled. "You should see what I did to him."

He pushed her knees apart so he could lean in and traced a finger down her neck, following the crusty stage bloodstain all the way to her cleavage. "I need to get a closer look."

"Um, so what do you think, Doc? Am I going to live?"

He placed his hand behind her head, lacing his fingers through her hair. "I don't know, dear, you've lost a lot of blood, and you're looking pretty pale... I think you might need mouth-to-mouth resuscitat—"

But he didn't get to finish because she had already clamped her lips onto his in a soul-searing kiss. She wrapped her legs around his waist as he crushed her to him and tasted her lips and tongue with urgency.

Knock, knock, knock. "Hurry up in there!"

Their kiss interrupted, they both laughed.

"Take me home. Now," she said, then downed the glass of wine.

"Nothing would make me happier."

He took her hand and, in no time, she was safely buckled in to the passenger side of his rented sedan, and they were on the road to her house.

They kissed at every red light they hit, then she fumbled and dropped her keys twice trying to unlock her front door. He scooped her in his arms, carried her down the hall, sat her on the bed, and kneeled in front of her and put his hands on the sides of her face.

"It's been a long time, Michael," she whispered.

"I know, sweetie. I know. Are you sure you want this?" he asked.

She reached over and turned the small reading lamp on. "Yep, I'm sure. And I want the light on."

"Lights on is good with me."

He took the doctor's coat off, dropped it to the floor, and then pulled the blue scrub shirt off over his head, tossing it to the side. She tentatively reached out and stroked his bare shoulders, then ran her hands down his chest.

He unlaced her boots, letting them drop to the carpet before pulling her to her feet. He reached his hand around and unzipped her dress and it fell loose and slipped off her shoulders. It slid over her bare breasts and down to the floor, and she stepped out of it. She stood to face him wearing only a small pair of pale pink lace panties and a nervous grin.

"You're beautiful," he said, then nodded toward the prosthetic gash on her neck. "But uh, you seem to be bleeding."

"Oh crap!" She put her hand over her fake neck wound.

"I'm kidding. Right now your whole body could be covered in zombie rot makeup, and I wouldn't care."

Elle blushed through the pale makeup on her face, but took the compliment as his gaze caressed her, lingering here and there.

"Why are you so far away?" she asked, reaching out to him.

He stepped forward, gathered her in his arms and

kissed her thoroughly. The feeling of their bare skin finally touching was excruciatingly delightful. She took his hand and placed it on her left breast, over her heart, which pounded below her warm velvet skin. She let out a soft moan, muffled into his mouth, as he backed her toward the bed.

She hesitated. "I hope this makeup won't stain my sheets. I should have washed it off. Maybe I should get a towel. Maybe I should…"

"Shhh. I'll buy you new ones if it does."

"Deal."

****

Michael laid back and held Elle tightly and protectively at his side, slowly caressing her shoulder with his fingers as their pulses slowed. Their lovemaking had been intense. He couldn't help himself and had taken her hard, sure and fast, but now regretted it was over so quickly.

As they lay there, her hand moved over his chest, her fingers toying with the sparse hair. She lifted her head to kiss his shoulder, then snuggled closer.

"Elle, you're amazing," he said.

After a moment, she burst out laughing, and he couldn't help but laugh, too.

"Well, don't go getting a big head or anything over it," he said, raising an irritated eyebrow at her. "I'm shutting up now. Apparently you have drained all my brain cells."

"So it's true then, men think with their cocks? I mean, if I drained your brain cells…" she said, letting her words trail off.

He looked over at her again, but before he could say anything she kissed him solidly on the mouth.

She leaned back and traced the outline of his lips with her finger then let her hand travel down the center of his chest to the flat plain of his stomach and below, under the sheet.

"Oh, what have we here?" she asked, her fingers encircling and sliding up and down his length.

He let out a long breath and closed his eyes as his erection grew under her steady, sensual strokes.

"I want you inside me again as soon as possible," she whispered in a low, honest voice, and she only had to say it once.

He turned to kiss her and laid her back on the pillow, her hair spilling around her face like a soft, glowing aura. Yes, he would make love to her again; only this time there would be no awkward, quick discussions about birth control, or overly nervous thoughts to complicate things. This time it would be different. It would be the first *real* time, with no hindrances.

She looked beautiful, even with some of the vampire makeup still on. He'd thought about bringing her into the shower, but decided he'd do it after. Right then and there, he had to have her again, and nothing was stopping him. He snaked his tongue down the hollow of her throat to the full curves of her breasts. It was hard to ignore the urge to thrust back into her right at that very second, but there was something else he wanted, and needed, to do first.

He edged down her stomach and settled between her thighs. He glanced up, meeting her half-lidded eyes briefly before covering her with his mouth. The sweet smell and taste of her under his tongue sharply heightened his own desire. Her fingers braided through his hair, and he felt her relax against him and soon she arched her back as the first set of shockwaves set in. But he didn't stop. Finally, after a second orgasm, she went limp under him, entirely his. All she could do was smile weakly as he kissed his way up her body again.

He grabbed her right buttock and entered her slowly. "I'm not finished with you yet," he said with no uncertainty. "I suggest you hold on. This might go on for a while."

She wrapped her legs around him and closed her eyes as he leaned down to graze her lips with his. They made love with earnest conviction, and he'd never felt that way during sex before. It seemed it would never be enough, and when they finally crested together, it was as if he had drowned at the hands of a siren.

It was at that moment he knew there was no way that he'd be able to accept the senior position at Steele if it meant he'd be away from her. He needed to be with her as often as possible.

They lay there for a while, spent and tired, but eventually he brought her into the shower to wash the makeup off before they went to sleep.

Sleeping next to Elle felt like the most natural thing in the world, and he stayed awake listening to her gentle breaths until he drifted to sleep as well.

At one point she murmured *"hmm"* in her sleep, and it sounded like the purr of a cat, which reminded him of the day he'd met her.

****

"This sucks!" Elle announced as they woke the next morning.

"Um, huh?" Michael replied, sitting up and trying to get a grasp on his bearings. He raked his hands through his hair. He was in Elle's bed and they were both naked. They'd made love and he'd spent the night, but now... "What sucks?"

"I can't be flying back and forth all the time. We live a thousand miles apart. Or more. Is it more? I don't even know. I mean, I like New York and all..."

"Wait, wait, wait, hold on there," Michael lay back down beside her and gathered her in his arms. "There's something you don't know yet."

"Hmm?" Her eyes implored him.

"I rented an apartment here."

"What? Really?" She leaned up on her arm to look at him. "But aren't you moving on to the next acquisition?"

"No, actually. I've got an apartment, and I plan to stay here for as long as it takes to make sure the new Stone Mountain gets off to a good start." He consciously left out the part about protecting them from John's corporate greed.

She frowned slightly and then smiled again, but the smile didn't reach her eyes. "That's great."

"You never asked me again where I was from."

"You're right. I guess, I just kind of forgot about it. So where are you from?"

"Born at St. Luke's Hospital, George Washington High School."

"Denver?"

He nodded.

"What? Seriously?"

He smiled. "Seriously. I moved to New York when I was twenty-two. My dad died ten years ago and Mom moved to Albany. Yes, Elle, my roots are here, too."

She smiled wide, but didn't say anything. Her eyes

became moist.

"Snuggle up and let me tell you about my experience growing up here," he said, gathering her in his arms. He proceeded to tell her of events his family had attended, doctors he had seen, favorite local restaurants, snowstorms and blizzards they had experienced, both from different sides of town.

Denver was a large city, but talking about their shared childhood experienced made it feel like a small town.

"Oh, speaking of The Eggery, are you hungry? I have breakfast stuff here, but for some odd reason I think I'm too tired to cook. It's my treat this time," Elle offered.

"Do they still make those enormous omelets?"

"Yep."

"Let's go, but we have to stop over at my place first. I don't want to wear hospital scrubs and a doctor coat."

"Good idea."

Chapter Fifteen

"Hey, I know this place. I had a friend that lived here. They have a great pool area," she said when they turned into this complex.

"Yeah, it came highly recommended from my college friend, Roger Benson."

"Roger Benson! Did he have a little sister named Sharla?"

Michael pulled his car into his spot and thought for a few moments before turning the engine off.

"Yeah, Roger does have a sister named Sharla. I actually dated her for a bit."

"You did? Oh my god, that was you? You were the guy that left her and went off to chiropractor school?"

"Guilty as charged." Michael wasn't sure how to gauge her reaction. Was she amused or angry that he'd split on her friend?

Elle laughed and he was relieved. Sheesh, he had to stop tensing up thinking she was going to react the way Sandra would have. She wasn't Sandra.

As they walked up to his door she said "Ha, I don't blame you for dumping her. Sharla was kind of a…well, she wasn't very fun to be around. I learned that pretty quickly. I met her while I was working at the sports memorabilia store at the mall."

"And she worked at the hot dog place."

"Correct! Wow, were we there at the same time?"

"Who knows? It's certainly possible since she didn't work there very long." Once inside, he grabbed her for another kiss. "We may have run into each other before. But now, I want to run into you all the time. On purpose." His hand traveled down to her butt. "And many multiple run-ins at once…naked."

"Hey, mister, right now you have to get dressed. I'm starved."

"Fine, fine. I'll be right back."

He tossed his keys and phone on the counter and headed off to the bedroom. Elle looked around the small sparsely furnished apartment. The walls were bare, as men's walls usually were, but he seemed to have everything he needed.

Michael's cell phone ringtone came on, and it vibrated off the edge of counter, landing face down on the carpet.

"Hey, can you check and see who that is?" he called from the bedroom.

"Okay." She bent down to pick up the phone and turned it over. Her heart sank and anger boiled.

"Uh, it's Sandra!" she called.

Oh, fucking wonderful.

She was supposed to call him that weekend with the names of some potential new ad clients for SMP. He quickly yanked a pair of jeans on, then pulled a hoodie over the long-sleeved gray thermal shirt he'd put on. He grabbed a pair of socks and tennis shoes and headed to the living room, not knowing what to expect.

Elle sat on the couch, looking at him expectantly. She handed his phone to him as he sat next to her.

"So, uh…" He wasn't sure how to go about telling her that Sandra was currently working at the same office he was. "Sandra got herself into a bind, and I'm helping her out a bit."

"Helping her out? Why? And how?"

"Because she doesn't have anyone else, and she's pregnant."

"What!"

"Not mine! Believe me I nearly had a heart attack, too."

"Okay, go on."

"I met up with her the day I dropped you guys off at the airport. I didn't want to go at first, you know, but she insisted. It turns out that she was laid off and was quite upset about it."

"Well, did they know she was pregnant?"

"I asked the same thing. And, no, they didn't. It was some shitty timing for her. Karma, maybe?"

"And the father, it's that realtor guy?"

"Yup."

"And he's not taking any responsibility for it, I'll bet. Is that why she came to you?"

"Actually, he did initially tell her he would help her and the baby out any way he could. Of course, at the time she didn't realize what he meant was he'd pay for an abortion."

"Oh jeez. What a wonderful guy."

"Exactly. So she wasn't having any luck finding a job because, well, because of her condition. She can't start a job and then, boom, tell them she's pregnant right after they hire her." He paused to reconsider. "I guess she could, but that would be the old her, not the new one."

"The *new* Sandra?"

"The pregnant Sandra. Pregnancy hormones must

Kay Phoenix

do something for the chemicals in her brain because she's actually been pretty pleasant to be around."

"Uh oh…"

"Well, she's not the Antichrist. I wouldn't have proposed to the Antichrist."

"I'd hope not. How often have you been around her lately, Michael?"

"She's working as an office assistant at Steele. I see her on the days I go in."

Elle pursed her lips. "Tell me more."

He explained the situation to her in more detail, and when he finished, he was relieved, feeling about fifty pounds lighter. She leaned over and wrapped her arms around him.

"I'm glad you helped her. You are a very nice man, Michael Williams. I'm a lucky girl."

He grabbed her hands and turned to face her. "No, I'm the lucky one. Believe me." Before he knew it, he'd laid her down on the couch, kissing her, and his hands were up her shirt undoing her bra. He realized she was hungry, but at the moment, so was he. For her.

"I think I can forgo food for another hour, maybe," she said, between breaths.

"How about two?" he asked and then hurriedly yanked the hoodie off, followed by his shirt.

Elle pulled her shirt off over her head and let it drop to the floor. "So are we staying on the couch?"

He glanced around. "Er, nope. Bed. Now."

They got into his bedroom and she wrapped her arms around him and said, "This time babe, it's my turn."

****

It was a little difficult for him to let her have

control at first, but he was willing to let it happen just the same. It had been a long time since he'd had *girl on top*. Sheesh, and he'd been bragging about lasting an hour or two. With this sexy woman on top, he'd be lucky if he lasted five minutes.

He had to concentrate.

She'd let him lie back on the bed and then crawled on top of him. She held his arms at his sides while she kissed and gently bit his neck and ears. The sensations traveled directly to the head of his dick, and he was dangerously hard. His erection strained against the zipper of his jeans as she edged her way down his chest, licking and kissing as she went. He actually wished he'd put underwear on as the zipper was scratchy and he had to be careful how he moved since his sensitive skin throbbed against it.

When she got to his waist, he expected to feel her unzip his jeans so his cock could be released and he could relax. But no, holy hell, she put her mouth over his jeans and blew out hot air. The feeling was one he'd never felt before. The heat from her breath warmed through his jeans, and if he thought he was hard before, now he was a brick. He wasn't hungry anymore. Matter of fact, he couldn't think about food or anything else. His mind was completely blank except for the...oh, now she was finally pulling his zipper down.

"Oh my," she said when she pulled him out of his pants. "Mmmm."

She licked the tip, then all the way down one side, and he tensed up.

"You okay?" she asked, and then licked him again.

"Oh, I'm better than okay, but you don't know what you're dealing with down there, babe. It could be…unpredictable."

"Fine by me." She took him in her mouth.

"Holy God," he sighed, then laid his head back and closed his eyes. Blow jobs were amazing, and it had been too long since his last one. Too long indeed, so long he was afraid it wouldn't be long before he finished. He squeezed his eyes shut. Then, she stopped. He opened one eye and saw that she'd climbed off the bed and was removing her pants.

"Condoms?" she asked.

Michael pulled his wallet out of his back pocket, took one out, then kicked his shoes away and yanked his jeans off. He tore open the packet and slid the condom on as she crawled back up on the bed and positioned herself above him. She took him in slowly, and it felt so good.

Elle maintained her rhythm, speeding up and grinding harder as her own release built deep inside her. He loved the breathy sounds she made and knowing it was him that caused her to make those sounds made it even better.

His own orgasm was rather…surprising. It didn't build up as usual; it just came. Yes, it came, and it was a hard one. He could hardly control himself and jolted for a bit afterward as if he'd been shocked by several hundred volts.

Elle looked satisfied with herself as she slid off of him, smiling like a cat.

"How was that?" she asked.

"I…uh…I think I need to sleep for the rest of the day now," he answered lazily.

"No way, mister." She gently smacked him on the leg, hopped out of bed and started to pull her clothes on. "Come on, we've got some omelets to eat and things to discuss, so put your clothes back on."

Chapter Sixteen

"So I have a little confession to make," Michael said, as he stabbed into his first real Denver omelet in many years.

"Uh oh, what's that?"

"I did a little, uh, research on you. Internet-wise."

Elle shrugged. "I supposed you found out about my days in a street gang and my ties to the drug cartel."

He laughed. "Yeah, I was going to ask about that another time. But I did find out about Duncan Land Development. Why is it you stepped down from their Board?"

Elle frowned and set her fork down.

"I didn't mean to upset you, but I'm just curious, especially since it's your birth parent's company and all."

"I didn't resign. They recently revamped their website and *they say* the web designer got confused because he couldn't find my name on their official list, so he left me out. See, in the Board Members section I'm listed as Gabrielle Duncan, but in the official roster, I'm Gabrielle Johnston, of course. Supposedly it's being fixed. Apparently it's not a top priority, since it's appeared that way for over a month now, but it's fine, really. I'm still on the board. I'm the only Duncan at Duncan Land Development."

"They need to make sure your name is back up

there. And pronto. Don't let them bully you."

"Agreed. So now it's my turn. I have things to discuss with you."

"Is that so? Somehow that doesn't surprise me. Okay, shoot."

"Well, it's mostly logistics. About the Living Dead show next week…"

"Yes, we need to get our flights all squared away."

"About that… I'll be in San Diego. I leave on Tuesday evening, and I'm supposed to come back on Friday morning."

"Not a problem. We can coordinate our flights on Friday so I arrive in New York before you, and I'll just stick around at the airport and wait."

"Perfect. Okay, no more to discuss. That was it."

"You're easy."

"You think? Maybe I should be tougher." She kicked him under the table, but not too hard.

"Please, no. I like you just the way you are."

She smiled and caressed his calf with her foot.

"I like you, too, Michael."

****

Friday morning came and Elle pulled the shade down on the plane's window. She'd declined an alcoholic beverage; still, she didn't want to have to be forced to look out the window and be reminded of how out of control her existence was at the moment.

Flying was…for the birds.

But she'd fly. She'd live through it and she had an exciting weekend to look forward to. In a few hours, she'd see Michael, and that evening they'd head to the concert and she'd finally meet the band backstage.

It wasn't until that moment she wondered how

Michael managed to score the tickets anyways, especially to get backstage. Those tickets couldn't have come cheap. She wondered if he'd purchased them specifically with her in mind, or if he had in fact been given them as some sort of thank-you for something, as he'd said. Either way, she was stoked.

But she was more stoked about seeing him. He hadn't left her mind for five minutes since when she'd left on Tuesday evening, and she wondered if he felt the same way. She had been dangerously close to telling him she loved him several times already, but it was way too soon for that.

Elle closed her eyes and let a daydream fill her mind. Soon, her head jerked, and she realized she'd actually fallen asleep for a few minutes. On a plane. That never happened before. The fact that she'd fallen asleep must mean something, but she wasn't sure what. She'd even gone to Australia once and been wide awake the entire flight.

An hour later, the plane started descending into New York to land at LaGuardia, which was the airport they would be meeting in. It was closer to his apartment and made more sense. As the plane circled Manhattan, she slowly pulled the shade up and peeked out the window. Below her, the city sprawled out in a gray vista reaching as far as she could see in either direction. But there was one giant swatch of green smack in the middle. Central Park.

Elle read once that park designers knew that even city dwellers needed a bit of green; thus, they pushed to make the park as large as they could. The size of it allowed local residents to visit a quiet sanctuary whenever they needed to. She'd also read articles stating there were families of deer and even a family of coyotes that had taken up residence in the park. It was nothing short of amazing. The plane made a wide turn directly above Central Park before it banked to land at LaGuardia.

Waiting for the other passengers to exit always got on Elle's nerves. She hated waiting. But the many New Yorkers on the flight were well versed in the value of a quick, efficient exit, so she didn't have to wait for long. She headed to baggage claim where her knight awaited. The wide smile on his face echoed her own as they embraced so long that the baggage carousel started moving before they let go. He kissed her, then they found a spot to stand near the carousel.

"So I figure we go back to my place, freshen up a bit, and then head into town. I'm sorry, but I have to stop in the office for a minute first. Then I have reservations at Don Antonio's for pizza."

"Mmm, sounds like a great idea. I'm looking forward to seeing your place." She squeezed his hand. "Oh, there's mine," she said as she pointed at her purple suitcase. He grabbed it.

Elle was impressed with the way he navigated the public transportation system of the city. They'd caught a train from the airport station and then exited near his apartment, which was only a short block from the train. His neighborhood looked just as she'd imagined and his Volt was parked in the driveway.

"I meant to ask...they have charging stations around here?"

"Of course. And in most of the car parks in the city."

"That's very interesting. Ron would love knowing

that." The words slipped out before she could stop them. She wasn't sure how Michael would react to her speaking of her deceased husband, but hoped it wouldn't be a problem. He'd been a big part of her life and would certainly come up in conversation now and then.

"Would he? I'd have to impress him with my knowledge of statistics regarding the hybrid cars, huh?"

She smiled. "Wouldn't take much, I'm sure."

They went in the outside door, and then headed up to his door upstairs. He unlocked it and said, "Welcome to my apartment."

Elle glanced around and it was nicer than she'd imagined it to be. He clearly preferred a sparse look, or what *she* called a sparse look. Other people referred to it as "clean lines."

"Make yourself at home. We should probably leave in about two hours to get everything done on time."

"Two hours to waste, hmm?" She walked to him and put her arms around his waist. "I can think of some perfectly good ways to waste two hours."

"I hoped you'd say that." He kissed her, then took her hand, brought her to his bedroom, and had her lie back on his brand new bed. Only he didn't tell her it was a brand new bed.

He had been looking forward to breaking it in.

****

Two hours later, after putting his new bed through a vigorous quality assurance testing session, Elle got showered and dressed. She wore an old Living Dead T-shirt she'd had since high school in hopes the singer would sign it for her. It was a bit faded, but she had many happy memories in that shirt. She wore torn jeans with the black spiked heels she'd worn to *Wicked*.

Michael wore jeans, converse tennis shoes and a plain black T-shirt.

They grabbed their jackets and headed out the door to the train station, hand in hand. He pointed out his gym, a Greek bakery and Al's Cleaners as they walked by.

When they arrived at his building a half hour later, he brought her inside Steele and introduced her to the few people they passed as they headed to his office.

A brunette approached them wearing a navy blue pencil skirt and tan-colored cardigan over a white dress shirt. Elle felt especially conspicuous in her concert attire.

"Elle, this is Sandra," he said as he introduced them.

"Hello." Sandra reached her hand to Elle and she took it. She was normally a pretty good reader of people, and she was almost surprised to not get a strange vibe from Sandra at all. Perhaps her imagination had made her seem worse than she was.

"Hi, nice to meet you."

"Likewise. Michael's been talking about you a lot."

"He has?" She glanced at Michael surprised to know he'd talked to his ex about her. It was comforting. He winked.

"There's Patrick now," he said under his breath. "Listen, ladies, if you'll excuse me, I need to see Patrick about something."

"Sure," they both said in unison.

"So Michael says you're going to the concert tonight?" Sandra motioned toward Elle's shirt.

Elle fumbled with the hem. "Yeah. Big fan since

high school. Hopefully I can get this old thing signed."

"That sounds fun. I'm sure you'll have a great time." She peeked over Elle's shoulder. "Oh, I've got to run. It was nice meeting you."

"Okay," was all Elle could summon to say, feeling somewhat confused by their short encounter. She felt a hand on her shoulder and turned. It was a beefy man in a light brown suit with dark hair and pockmark scars on his cheeks. She guessed it was John.

"John Steele," he introduced himself and took her hand. He gave her a lingering once-over, and didn't even try to hide the fact that his eyes lingered in places they shouldn't have. Also he held her hand a little too tight and didn't seem to want to let go.

"Hi John, I'm—"

"I know who you are. You were supposed to be here an hour ago. What took you so long?"

"Um, excuse me? We took the subway, and I wasn't aware that we were supposed to be here earlier."

"When I called, I requested you be here at three. Not four." His tone was low and steady, and he held her hand tighter still.

"I'm sorry. I'm confused."

"Confused? You'll be sorry later when I call your boss. You were supposed to wait for me in the lobby."

"Huh?" Now he was scaring her. She tried to pull her hand away, but he still held it exceedingly tight. "I don't understand."

Michael approached him from behind alongside a shorter man that had very curly dark hair. He put his hand on his shoulder.

"John, I see you've met Elle," he said.

John finally released his grip. Elle rubbed her hand.

"Elle?" John asked.

"Yeah, Elle Johnston, from Denver."

"Oh, shit. I thought you were someone else." John laughed and reached out to shake her hand again, but she wouldn't let him. She still rubbed her sore wrist.

"Uh, what did I miss?" Michael asked, his tone deepening.

John didn't say anything.

"He thinks I'm someone else who was supposed to meet him in the lobby an hour ago."

****

Michael saw stars. His uncle thought Elle was a *hooker?*

Apparently he had, and that was the last straw.

His fists clenched, his jaw stiffened, and his forehead furrowed as he struck his uncle across the face with the hardest punch he'd ever thrown. Then, when John fell to the ground, he went in for another one, and another. All he saw was red until he felt someone pulling him off of John.

"Michael. Michael, calm down. Calm down. There, that's it."

Fist still clenched, he looked around and saw it was Patrick trying to calm him. Elle's mouth was wide open, staring back and forth between him and the man on the ground that bled from his nose.

Sandra walked up behind Elle and touched her shoulder. "Are you okay? Holy crap, what happened?"

"I'm not entirely sure."

A small crowd had started to gather.

"Hey, what's that?" someone asked, and pointed to a small plastic bag on the ground next to John. Patrick leaned down and picked it up. There was a white powdery substance inside it. He promptly put it right back down in the same spot.

Just then, the lobby elevator dinged and a tall blonde in platform heels and a too-short skirt walked down the hall, her heels clicking with each step. Upon seeing everyone who was standing around look up at her, she backed up a few steps.

The receptionist, who had joined the crowd, stepped forward. "Can I help you?"

"I'm looking for John Steele," the woman answered.

"Well, there he is." The receptionist moved to the side to display John's big form sprawled out on the floor in his brown suit like a baked potato. "Can I ask what your business was? I don't have anything on his books."

"It's of a personal nature. I was supposed to be here at three, but my train was late," the woman answered. "You know what, you all look busy. I think I'll head out and see him another time." She backed away and disappeared into the elevator.

"Oh my god, that was a prostitute!" Sandra said, a bit loudly.

"It was," Michael agreed. He went to Elle and put his arms around her.

John moaned and moved a bit on the floor. Michael had to try hard not to kick him.

Patrick turned to Michael. "I'll straighten everything out here. You guys get out of here. Go to dinner and your show. Enjoy yourselves. Forget about this bullshit."

Michael was glad to leave. His hand hurt and the surge of adrenaline was giving him a headache.

"I don't even understand what just happened," Elle said when they were in the elevator alone. "But I know that whatever it was, it must have been building up for some time."

"It has. He's a fuck-up, John is. He has a bad habit with call girls. And cocaine, apparently. He's taken a turn for the worst in the last year. He's been missing meetings. Generally screwing up a lot."

"I see. So now, it seems everyone knows."

"Everyone knew before. This is nothing new, but I couldn't control my anger when I realized he thought you were his order of the evening."

She touched his shoulder. "That was very gallant of you."

"You know, I'm not even worried. He can't press charges against me. There'd be no way they'd hold up. He can't fire me, either. Patrick already told me there's a group that wants me to take over for John, so I know they'd stand behind me."

"I'm sure, whatever happens will be what was meant to happen." Elle squeezed his other hand. "How's your hand? I saw you rubbing it."

"It's fine, but sore. He was squeezing it pretty tight, and wouldn't let go. It was pretty creepy."

The elevator doors opened and they stepped into the main lobby of the building, where John's escort was supposed to have met him.

Michael pulled Elle to the side. "Did he hurt you? Do you want to press charges against him?" he asked quietly.

"Charges? No."

"Are you sure?"

"Yeah, I'm sure. Besides, isn't he your family?"

"Yes, but you understand how this is a big deal, right? He assaulted you, and you're one of our clients. A thing like this could potentially ruin us."

"Of course I understand, that's why I don't want to press charges."

Michael let out a long breath. "Okay. But something has to happen. We'll figure it out. It can't go on with him the way it has."

Michael finally felt his adrenaline start to wear off, but his fist still throbbed as they sat through a somewhat awkward dinner. He received a text message, so he pulled out his phone and checked it.

"John came to and started raving like a lunatic. The police took him away. It's been an interesting evening. Enjoy your show." Michael laughed out loud and handed the phone to Elle so she could read it.

"Interesting, for sure," she said.

Later during the concert he received another text message from Patrick. *"John called Rick to represent him. That white powder in the bag was cocaine, and he also had some in his wallet. Can you believe it? He's not coming back. Have a great night, boss."*

Michael thought he'd wait to let Elle read that one when the show was over. She was dancing and having too much fun. And he was having too much fun watching her, especially when she got to meet the singer and have him sign her shirt. She was giddy, and seeing her happy made him happy.

As they left, she was still reeling in the fun she'd had when he handed his phone over for her to read the message.

"Wow! And, what does he mean, 'boss?'"

"I guess we'll see."

Elle became quiet.

"What is it?"

"I'm just wondering. If you take over John's spot, does that mean you will have to be here more often?"

"Maybe. But let's not think about that right now.

"Okay. One day at a time." The rest of their walk to the station and the subway ride was quiet, though she held his hand and laid her head on his shoulder. He kissed the top of her head.

As they slipped into bed that night, Elle spoke, "You know what? We can make it work. If you need to be here, then you need to be here. It's what you have to do."

It was the reassurance he needed to hear. He pulled her close and held her tight. He knew he never wanted to let her go.

****

Early the next week, when they were back in Denver, Michael took a call from Patrick relaying the information that the police had found cocaine in John's system.

"It's official, he's is going to jail without passing Go. Jesus, can you believe it? If New York's prostitution laws are lenient, their drug laws aren't. He's going away for a long time!"

"Wow. Just, wow…" Michael exclaimed. He was at a loss for better descriptive words as even though he knew his uncle was a scumbag; he couldn't believe they found cocaine on him and in his blood.

"So I guess the corner office is yours then, Michael."

Michael knew exactly what to say. "Unless you claim it first. I think you have a thousand-mile head start on me."

He could almost hear Patrick smile.

"Patrick?" he asked when he didn't hear an answer.

"Yeah, I'm walking to the train right now. I figure I'll get there at least a few days ahead of you." He laughed. "No, only kidding. It's yours. We'll talk soon. It's all good."

Michael hung up and smiled.

It was going to be a very good day.

Michael was in a very good mood, but was nervous to tell Elle the news. He waited for her by her Jeep at the college. When she approached him, she slowed her steps and studied him warily.

"What's up? What's that look about?" she asked.

"You are looking at the proud new CEO of a midsized business investment firm."

"You did? I mean, you are? That's great! Congratulations!" She threw her arms around him and he spun her around.

"It'll be a new adventure for sure. But there's one thing I'm wondering. See, I don't want to do it alone. I need to know that you will be with me. Even if you still live here, I have no problem flying out every weekend to see you, or vice versa. I only know I can't be without you. I love you."

Tears welled in her eyes. "I will. And I can't be without you, either. I love you, too."

A word about the author...

Ms. Phoenix is a rare bird herself, a lifelong resident of Las Vegas, Nevada. She belongs to Las Vegas Romance Writers and has served on the board. She is also a member of Romance Writers of America with PRO status.

Prior to writing, Kay was a graphic artist for fifteen years in the casino industry and holds degrees in both Graphic Arts and Psychology. In her spare time she enjoys hiking, camping and photography. Her art and photography are displayed in Las Vegas art galleries several times a year.

Kay writes in the contemporary and paranormal romance categories, as well as non-fiction articles. Please visit her website at:

www.KayPhoenix.com.

Thank you for purchasing
this publication of The Wild Rose Press, Inc.

If you enjoyed the story, we would appreciate your
letting others know by leaving a review.

For other wonderful stories,
please visit our on-line bookstore at
www.thewildrosepress.com.

For questions or more information
contact us at
info@thewildrosepress.com.

The Wild Rose Press, Inc.
www.thewildrosepress.com

Stay current with The Wild Rose Press, Inc.

Like us on Facebook

https://www.facebook.com/TheWildRosePress

And Follow us on Twitter
https://twitter.com/WildRosePress

www.ingramcontent.com/pod-product-compliance
Lightning Source LLC
Chambersburg PA
CBHW051519170626
46811CB00002B/906